THE BACK ROADS
Of
TERROR

By

CHRISTOPHER MALINGER

ISBN – 13: 978-0990701811
ISBN – 10: 0990701816

DEDICATION

This book is dedicated to all my children
and grandchildren, who, without their knowledge,
have given me my inspiration for tales of fantasy and horror.

CONTENTS

ACKNOWLEDGMENTS

Eileen Malinger
Jonathan Malinger
Therese Y. Gaudette
Tom Bender
and
To all my teachers, both past and present,
who have assisted me as a writer, I thank you.

Cover Design by Eileen Malinger

Photo credit: andreluc88/Shutterstock.com

A MITCHELL STREET STORY

George Milton slowly dismounted the streetcar on 8th and Mitchell. He stood motionless as the trolley passed in front of him. The blur of the vehicle faded and his gaze fell on the apartment building door across the street. The long fingers of the approaching evening's shadows stretched toward the building and were met by the light from his apartment window. He didn't want to cross, but forcing his feet to move, he stepped onto the brick-lined pavement.

He had left his job at the defense plant much earlier than usual. Now he had to face his wife Elizabeth with the news that he was fired. As he walked slowly toward the door, the events of the last few hours replayed in his mind. His boss was hard on him. Singled him out, constantly pushed him to work harder and faster. Finally in the heat of an argument, words were exchanged and George responded with a forceful push that sent his supervisor sprawling to the floor. The result was his immediate dismissal.

George would normally walk kitty-corner to his apartment, but this time he made the trip by touching each of the street corners, like a baseball player rounding the bases to home. The floor creaked beneath his feet as he stepped into the hallway leading to the stairs. He looked up at the stairwell and pushed the switch button that activated a solitary bulb, shedding a faint glow, barely illuminating the way. Each step upward produced a telltale sound of his approach, but was masked by the muffled clatter coming from the apartment above.

He reached the top flight and turned left toward his apartment; Elizabeth still unaware of his approach. Drawing closer to the door he heard her and his two children over the sound of the "Green Hornet" on station WCFL. No doubt she was trying to get the kids to be quiet so she could hear the show. It was sometime after 5:30 and it was Elizabeth's favorite radio program.

When he turned the doorknob and entered the kitchen his wife had a look of surprise, startled by his approach, which was veiled by the clamor of kids and the radio. He was early too. She abruptly wiped her hands on the kitchen towel that hung over the sink. Drying them further on her flower-patterned apron, she turned toward him. She sensed something was wrong and checked her advance.

Elizabeth knew her boundaries with George. He was a loving husband, but at times could fly into a fit over seemingly nothing. He also possessed a jealous streak that proved embarrassing at times when they were in public.

He closed the door with his back and remained leaning against it. The bag he was holding dropped to the floor. It made a thud as it hit the floor. Still angled against the door he told his wife, who also was in a state of suspension, of being fired. Her eyes began to well up as she heard the news. Before his arrival she had been in good spirits because the two of them planned to go to a movie that night. It was something she always enjoyed doing. They were going to the Wisconsin Theater to see "Let's Face It" staring Bob Hope and Betty Hutton. Because of the demand, the theaters were open late to accommodate the full wartime crew of factory workers, and their need for recreation. She instantly knew their plans just changed.

George walked over to the kitchen table and pulled out a wooden chair, which squealed as it moved over the worn linoleum. He slumped onto its unpadded seat. After a moment he bent forward, cradling his head onto his forearms that rested on the table. Staying in that position for several tense moments he suddenly shot straight up and let the chair fly backward onto the floor. His quick movement startled Elizabeth and his two children, Matthew and Mary.

Mary was youngest of the two, only three years old compared to Matthew who was five. George hoped they could someday afford a small house and get away from city life; in his present state of mind, a seemingly impossible dream. To him his life was ruined and the future appeared hopeless. Not only did he lose his job, but he also feared the legal consequences to his action. Anyone who harmed the war effort could face jail time. Even if that didn't happen, could he find another job after this incident? His head reeled with fear, which turned to depression. Nothing was made sense.

Action had to be taken, he thought, nearly knocking over Elizabeth as he brushed past her on his way to the bedroom. He was in search of the Luger that he bought years earlier as a home-defense weapon. The sound of moving drawers intermingled with several thuds alerted his wife of danger and the hairs at the nape of her neck stood in fearful apprehension of what would follow.

George emerged from the bedroom with a look that Elizabeth had never seen. It was wild, a piercing and menacing glare that made her clench her hands to her breast and retreat a step.

"What are you going to do with that gun, George? "She asked him with a trembling resonance in her voice.

"I'm going to kill that son-of-a-bitch. He kept riding me and now my life is ruined. Our life is ruined! I will fix his life too," he stammered.

That was George's logic, or lack of. She couldn't believe her ears at his ramblings and told him to put the gun back and forget his insane plan. Something indeed had snapped in him, for now he didn't hear anything she said. Elizabeth's words echoed in his brain but did not have form or meaning. His ears felt like they were going to burst. She took a few steps forward and put out a hand to grab the pistol.

"Give me that gun!" she demanded.

George reacted by jerking his hand away from her grasp while tugging on the trigger. The gun became leveled at Mary who sat calmly in the highchair behind Elizabeth.

Suddenly Mary's face exploded and her blood and tissue became an odd addition to the pale green paint of the kitchen wall. Elizabeth became hysterical and Matthew started to scream. At that moment the kitchen door opened. Becky, the baby sitter who lived down the hall, stood motionless in the doorframe. Becky was going to watch the kids for the night so George and Elizabeth could go to the movies. Color fled from her face and she began to emit a strange squeal at the scene before her. She soon became silent when George aimed and fired his gun a second time. The bullet from his Luger found its mark in the center of her chest. Her body convulsed and tumbled backwards into the hallway.

George, no longer present in mind, became an animal reacting to movement and sound. He fired two shots in rapid succession at Elizabeth who crouched defensively over Matthew with her slender body. The rounds entered her back, continued into the quivering body of Matthew, who was crying uncontrollably. The crying stopped.

The carnage was over and silence shared space with the smoke-filled kitchen. George suddenly became aware of the terror he had inflicted on his family as he stared in shock at the aftermath of his deeds. He started to sob. Slowly he put the pistol to his head and squeezed the trigger. He heard a click; the room with all its horror remained.

The gun had misfired. Had it failed on the first pull of the trigger this may not have happened and he may have come to his senses. He continued to weep violently. The pressure in his head became explosive and the shaking hand that held the pistol dripped with sweat. His whole body shook. Pulling back the charging handle of the firearm he ejected the misfired round and refreshed the chamber. Trembling, he held the gun to his temple again. This time he didn't hear the gun's report. It was over and his bloody body collapsed onto the floor.

***

In a span of less than one hour an entire family ceased to exist along with one unsuspecting young girl. People talked about the events for several years because of the sensational nature of the crime. From the aftermath a tale was spawned, backed by mysterious happenings. The crime, so vicious, it left an evil residue imbedded in the very framework of the upper floor.

All the apartments remained vacant—the landlord unable to rent them. First because of the fear of living in a place associated with murder, and a murder most gruesome at that. The other reason was the hauntings.

No one could stay in the apartments because of the specter that plagued the rooms. Loud noises with the sound of slamming doors relentlessly troubled any tenant, who unfamiliar with the events, unwittingly rented, their tenanted period brief.

Eventually one person occupied the second floor. His name was Iggy, a somewhat down-and-out holdover from the days of vaudeville. Iggy, the exception, through madness and economics remained. He stayed pretty much to himself, occasionally visiting the clothing store below. If prompted, he would relive old burlesque numbers that included splits and pratfalls, much to the delight of the store's patrons and employees.

At one point in his career Iggy had been onstage with Jimmy Durante. At Christmas time, he would profess his past association by hanging a sign in his apartment window, facing Mitchell Street. It read "Merry Christmas from Iggy and Jimmy Durante." Being a bit of an eccentric and this association with the past gave him an identity that could not be discarded any more than one might remove himself from his own shadow.

Iggy eventually died peacefully in his sleep. After his passing the entire second floor with all its history was turned into warehouse space for the clothing store below. Iggy's spirit refused to move on. He was the counterbalance to George's wickedness and felt obliged to remain out of gratitude to the owner's generosity. It was his way of repaying him for living there almost rent-free.

As a spirit, Iggy had more control of the situation. The tempo of the hauntings increased after his passing, but no one knew the real cause. It was a fight between good and evil. The banging of doors, the sound of gunshots mixed with boxes mysteriously tumbling to the floor became more intense.

On one occasion Michael, the clothing storeowner's son went upstairs to fetch a case of slacks. Because of its size he brought along Chet, another employee, to help him.

"What's that noise?" Michael asked.

"Don't know," replied Chet. "It sounds like a radio. It's coming from the front storage room."

After opening the door, the sound ceased. Michael reached for the light switch and illuminated the interior. Neatly labeled boxes of clothing rested on large folding tables, occupying the room's perimeter. Heavy drapes covered the two windows facing Mitchell Street, allowing only a sliver of light to frame the curtains. There was a radio, disconnected and sitting on a shelf near the door. The only other electrical device was an old floor fan, standing motionless in the center of the room; also unplugged. Iggy's unseen spirit reclined comfortably on top of an empty table. Iggy smiled at his diversion, not capable of anything more mischievous than spooking someone.

Neither Michael nor Chet saw anything. The light was extinguished and they warily resumed their task.

The hauntings with the bumping and thumping continued sometimes accented with an occasional shriek or squeal. Some noises could not be identified because they forgot what splits and pratfall sounded like. The phantom giggle that followed was recognized though, driving chills down the spine of any employee, and with it, a rapid retreat.

Like yin and yang the spirits were at odds. The owner of the building had other ideas and wanted whatever spirit or spirits to terminate their unworldly occupancy. Determined to purge the second floor of its unwelcome residents, and being Jewish, he enlisted the help of a Rabbi.

One evening, after the clothing store closed for the night, the Rabbi formed a ten-man quorum called a Minyan [meen-yahn]. They gathered in the center room of the second floor warehouse and formed a large circle.

Anticipating a change in the air, both George Milton and Iggy now moved outside the circle of men, each remaining opposite of each other. Like two men in a wrestling ring they orbited the gathering.

Candles were lit and the men joined the Rabbi in reciting Psalms 20 and 90, imploring the ghost or ghosts to move on. Finishing their prayers with, "And let the brightness of the Lord our God be upon us; and direct the works of our hands over us; yea, the work of our hands do you direct."

The final touch was the addition of Jewish amulets made from crystals hung in the three windows that faced west. With that, the group dispersed.

Their cleansing rite proved successful, of a sort. On that very night one of the candles was carelessly placed on a table near a rack of clothing. Fed by an unworldly breath, the partially extinguished candle sparked to life and ignited the cotton/linen-blended material. The smoldering clothing fell to the floor. It flamed up as it came in contact with a cloth, which rested on top of a container of solvent used to clean clothing. The accelerant ignited in a flash. It wasn't until someone noticed the orange glowing windows silhouetting the suspended amulets, before the alarm was sounded.

By the time the fire department arrived the building was spouting flames and belching smoke. The one-alarm fire turned into two as the glowing embers danced from one shelf to another within the building. Sputtering flames and long burning rivers of molten synthetics dripped to the floor obscured by heavy, dense, black smoke.

George Milton walked through the inferno on his way to places new. Iggy danced among the flames doing splits and pratfalls in celebration of his freedom. He even giggled, as some of the firemen would later attest to hearing, but others would claim it was only the sizzle of blazing wood

– nothing more.

I LOVE MY PUGGLE

I've never seen a dog like this. What kind is it?" asked Mildred, as she continued to lightly scratch the puppy behind its floppy ears.

"It's a puggle, a designer dog, which we recently acquired," the pet storeowner said with pride, "a crossbreed between a beagle and a pug."

"He's so cute and look at those big eyes. I think he likes me," Mildred mused.

"How much?" she asked, with a bit of apprehension in her voice. She was a widow with a limited income and any purchase, besides the necessities, had to be carefully considered.

"Only five hundred dollars," the man quickly said, adding, "But the companionship value far exceeds the monetary cost."

"Hmm—I'm not sure I can really afford the—" her words were quickly cut off by the salesman.

"A dog like this normally sells for around fifteen hundred dollars, and because I like you, I tell you what. I'll make it four-fifty, and drop off a large bag of dog food tomorrow at your apartment."

Swept away by the seemingly terrific deal, reduction in price, and the emotional bond already established, she agreed. After buying a dog chew, collar, leash, a small doggy bed, and water dish, she nevertheless had to write a check for almost five hundred dollars.

She received reassurance from the shop owner that the additional items would be delivered tomorrow, along with the food. Mildred eagerly accepted the cardboard pet carrier, beaming with delight as she exited the store.

The decision to buy a dog was not on her to-do list. In fact, she never went this way during her weekly trips to the library. Her routine outing usually resulted in obtaining a couple of books, which would serve as her entertainment, in addition to her favorite television shows. Now, out of nothing more than the desire to seek an alternative path home, she balanced books in one hand, and a boxed puppy in the other. With and look of contentment, she maneuvered her way through a stream of people.

Reaching her three-story brownstone she noticed several boxes sitting on the top landing, blocking the front door. Holding the cardboard pet carrier in her right hand, she shifted the books from her left side to the right, compressing them between her arm, and body. Grabbing the concrete railing with the freed left hand for support, she pulled her way to the top of the ten steps.

"Oh my, that was fast," she said, noticing the packages were for her. Three boxes formed a cardboard pyramid, with the name of the pet shop clearly labeled, "Designer Dogs" superimposed over an interlocking drawing of double D's.

She was as excited as a school child while she impatiently unlocked the front entrance. Her apartment was to the left, which she also eagerly unbolted. She placed the books inside on a nearby table. After depositing the pet carrier on the tiled floor, her first action was to immediately open the box, and then look at her new companion.

"Oh you are a cutie," her words directed at her tan fluffy treasure. "I'll have to give you a special name, but first things first. I need to bring in your stuff."

She scampered between entrance, and flat until all the boxes were inside. Taking off her coat she bent down, retrieved the puggle, and then retired to a padded oak rocking chair. The padding, long compressed through years of use, had a flowery pattern that also revealed wear. Her body eased into its indentation as she cuddled her furry puppy between her aged hands, and lap.

"Now what should we call you?" she deliberated. "Maybe you should be called Puggy?" The pup eyed her with affection as it cocked its head to one side. "No! I am going to call you Charlie, after my husband. Yes, Charlie you will be."

This was not Mildred's first dog. Both she and her late husband had several when they were married. Later, when they retired, and after the death of their last dog, they did some traveling. They did not want the responsibility of having a dog to care for. So, she was not unfamiliar with the needs and training of a puppy. After feeding him, she prepared his bed and set newspapers around its boundary to begin the process of paper-training the pup. She also tethered him to the adjacent radiator pipe, making sure he wouldn't go beyond the limits of the paper.

It was a long and exciting day for Mildred. Securing her new pet, she prepared herself for bed. Moving about her apartment she hummed a tune, now visibly comfortable with her decision to adopt a dog.

***

The sun streamed onto her bed as she awoke the next day, displaying a broken pattern of light from the partially opened blinds. Her sleep had been unbroken, devoid of any whining, or nocturnal barking, which surprised her, knowing puppies usually needed time to adjust to their new surroundings. Stretching in place, she slid from under the covers and firmly planted her feet into the open ends of her tan Chandra scuff slippers. She grabbed her robe from the foot of the bed, and began to wrap it around herself as she went toward the kitchen. Nearing the door, she heard tiny puppy yaps. She began to beam.

Once Mildred made eye contact with her new puppy both of them displayed gladness in seeing each other. Mildred bent over to untether him, and saw a couple of wet spots on the newspapers. This telltale sign gave evidence that his training had begun. She also saw something she wasn't expecting, a roll of what appeared to be money near the outer edge of the paper.

"What's this?" she said as she retrieved the tube of bills, before grabbing Charlie. "Did you get into something while I was sleeping?"

She held the money in one hand, and her dog in the other hand, while walking toward her rocking chair. After getting comfortable, she nested her pup on her lap, and closely examined the currency. Sliding off a loosely secured rubber band, she counted out ten new fifty-dollar notes.

The dog began to lick at both the money, and Mildred's hands, eagerly begging for attention. Mildred cupped the bills in her hand, and slid them into her right robe pocket. She held her dog up at eye level, and said, "If only you could speak."

Determining the source of the money was a mystery to her. One thing she knew, it did not belong to her. Most of her money was directly deposited in the bank, never allowing too much cash on hand. The income from stocks, bonds, and modest pension proceeds were directly deposited through automatic transactions. The rent, utilities, and insurance, were likewise handled electronically. Her late husband did all this to help minimize financial concerns before his passing.

She did not feel comfortable with all that cash around her apartment. After her breakfast, she decided to make a deposit in her bank, and at the same time take her new puppy for a walk.

Mildred cautiously guided herself down along the outside railing while her dog eagerly tugged on his leash. As she reached street level, her neighbor from across the hall approached her. She seemed to be returning from a shopping trip by the number of bags dangling from her hands.

"Good morning Mildred," Stella hailed, who appeared to eye the dog with some apprehension. "I see you have a little friend. Is it yours or are you watching it for someone?"

Mildred's smile faded a bit. "No, it's mine. I bought him yesterday. *Charlie,* and I are going for a little walk," she replied, visibly annoyed by the probing question.

"Well, I hope he won't be keeping you up at night by barking," Stella said in a saccharine tone while looking at the dog for any sign of aggression.

"He is a good boy, and I doubt he will make any more noise than your cat," Mildred snapped back, and began to resume her pace. "Have a nice day, Stella," she said in passing. "Busybody," she mumbled, once beyond earshot.

The annoyance with her neighbor wore off as she made her way toward the bank. Sometimes she would stop, pick up her dog and bond with him, which allowed Charlie a brief respite from the walk. Having reached her destination, Mildred lifted him into her arms and pushed her way through the entrance door. Once inside she saw little activity, and quickly found an open teller.

"Good morning, Mrs. Peterson," chimed the teller. "What is this? You appear to have a new friend. What's his name?" Her interest seemed to be sincere, and Mildred's reaction to her questions was warmly received.

"His name is Charlie, and he is my new baby," she proudly replied as if she were showing off her own child. Mildred never had any children; showering affection on pets, when her husband was alive, filled that gap.

Aware of the attention he was receiving. He responded by emitting a little whine, which brought a smile to both Mildred, and the teller.

"So, what can we do for you today?" the clerk asked.

"I would like to deposit some money into my checking account," she answered, while slipping ten fifty-dollar bills in her direction.

After receiving her deposit receipt she said goodbye, walked outside and turned left, in the direction of the pet shop. She wanted to see if she could get something special for her new sweetie—perhaps another dog chew.

Charlie continued to lead, as if by instinct, knowing the way. During the entire trip he exhibited uncanny intelligence. As they approached the pet store's location Mildred became disoriented, and suddenly lost. The spot where the shop was located, or, rather where it should have been, was occupied by a candy store. She paused, and looked around trying to find her bearings. Everything was in order except the presence of the confectionary shop, which seemed to have replaced the pet store. Mildred entered the shop.

"I'm sorry lady, you can't bring that dog in here," the man in a white uniform shouted across the empty store. "It's against health department rules," he added, this time a bit more gently.

"Oh, that's okay; I wanted to ask you a question. I'll stay here by the door." Before giving him an opportunity to refuse her request she said, "What happened to the pet store that was here yesterday?"

The man in white remained behind the counter, but moved closer to the entrance. He eyed her with some suspicion. "Lady, I have been here nearly five years, and don't know anything about a store that sells animals. Perhaps you are mistaken? There is one a couple of blocks away on 27th Street," he told her while resting both arms on top of the white metal countertop. Below him, and visible through the glass facings of the cabinet stood rows of chocolate, enticing any would-be-customer to purchase the sweet delicacies.

The tempting aroma of the store's interior made Mildred realize that she was getting hungry. The dog's squirming, also prompted her that he was getting impatient, and wanted his freedom.

"Thank you very much. I'll be on my way," she said, and pushed her way through the glass door, and onto the sidewalk. Once outside, she bent down to let her dog have its liberty again. Before she could set him down he sprang from her arms, eagerly making contact with the cement walkway. Already knowing the way, he pulled Mildred in the direction towards home.

"You are a smart one," she said, amazed by the dog's sense of direction.

As she neared her apartment Mildred noticed a police car parked in front. "I wonder what that is all about?" she said out loud. Charlie only sounded out a small yelp, and increased his strain on the tether.

Approaching the front hallway, Mildred came face-to-face with a policeman who had just left Stella's apartment. "Good afternoon ma'am," the officer said as he helped hold the door for her, and her dog.

Stella was standing in her own doorway when she exclaimed, "I've been robbed! It isn't safe to live here anymore."

"Excuse me, Mrs. ah—" the officer began.

Mildred interrupted, "My name is Mildred, Mildred Peterson. I live right here," she pointed in the direction of her apartment. "What's this all about?"

"It appears that your neighbor was robbed sometime last night. Would you mind answering some questions?"

"Oh, no! Sure, officer. What do you want to know?"

"First of all did you see, or hear, anything unusual last night? Anything unusual?" the patrolman emphasized.

"No, nothing at all. I went to bed at my normal time, around ten o'clock. I'm a sound sleeper," Mildred said while trying to keep Charlie from jumping on the policeman's trousers.

"I believe your neighbor was the victim of a robbery," the officer reported, while glancing at the dog's antics.

"What was stolen, Stella?" Mildred asked, switching her gaze to her distraught neighbor.

"Five hundred dollars! It was hidden among my linens, all rolled up in a rubber band. Now it's all gone. I saw the money yesterday when I was rearranging my drawers. Who would do such a thing?"

The announcement of the loss, and description caused Mildred to shift in place. Noticeably shaken by the news, she averted her eyes from Stella to her dog. Her glance was brief, returning her attention to the officer.

"I'm sorry officer, that's all I can tell you." Mildred asked, "Will that be all? I have to get my dog fed, and I need something to eat, too."

"No, that will be all. Here is my card, Mrs. Peterson. You can call me if you should think of anything else." Mildred accepted the card and quickly unlocked her door. Retreating from the hallway, she eagerly sought the safety of her place and freedom from uncomfortable questions.

"Well, Charlie, it would seem that you have some explaining to do," she said staring at him with searching eyes. "I don't believe in coincidences. I also don't believe in dogs being able to go through walls, and doors, but my intuition tells me you are somehow involved." She sternly scolded her new puppy, not giving him any consideration of innocence in the matter. He appeared to understand, yet displayed little remorse. In fact his throaty growl appeared a bit defiant.

Keeping her eyes fixed on him, she said, "We are going back to the bank tomorrow, withdraw that money, and find a way to give it back to Stella."

***

"Good morning, Mrs. Peterson, what brings you back so soon?" the bank teller asked, noticeably surprised by the visit.

"I—I made a mistake. I have to—withdraw that money from yesterday. Something unexpected came up." The unusual behavior and stammering caused the clerk some concern.

"Are you all right Mrs. Peterson?"

"Yes, fine dear. This little fella kept me up last night and I guess I'm a little tired."

Once home, Mildred needed to find a way to slip the money back into Stella's apartment. She was uncertain if she was up to the task. "How am I going to get this back to her?" she asked, while looking at her new dog for answers.

Contemplating a solution to her dilemma she exclaimed, "I know. You can take it back to her. The same way you stole it, Charlie."

That night before going to bed, Mildred took the roll of bills, firmly secured by a rubber band, and left them outside the tethered reach of her dog. Mildred contemplated leaving him untied, but if he was able to take the money while being tied before, then he could put it back too. Before going to bed she petted him, and said, "Now, you do the right thing tonight. Okay?" His look was not reassuring, as he cocked his head to one side, licking the air with his tongue.

***

When morning came the money remained in the exact spot Mildred left it. The puppy, alert, and begging to be held, reared up on his hind legs straining against the leash. Once again she picked up the bills, and her dog, and retired to her rocking chair.

After petting him behind the ears she rolled him over to give him a belly rub. "What's this? It looks like blood. Did you hurt yourself?" she asked while examining his body for any possible wounds. She found none.

Mildred went to the kitchen cabinet, and retrieved an old washrag from under the counter. After soaking it in water she used it to wipe his underbelly, and removed the pinkish discoloration from his hair.

After cleaning him up, she began her day's routine by feeding him, then taking care of herself. As she was beginning to prepare her breakfast she heard a commotion coming from across the hall.

When she opened the door she saw Stella, grim-faced, eyes sunken with grief, holding a black trash bag. It appeared heavy as the folds of the plastic bag pulled taut from her grip.

"Is everything okay, Stella?" she asked thoughtfully.

"It's Chester. He's dead," her words strained in mourning the loss.

"How did he die?"

"I found him in the bathroom, all bloodied. Something killed him." Her words brought a surge of tears. "First my money is stolen—now Chester is dead," she babbled between swells of grief.

"Something killed him?" Mildred asked, looking for clarification of the word "something."

Mildred went to help Stella with the bag. Between the two of them, they managed to deposit the dead cat in the trashcan in the front alcove, beneath the staircase.

"Did something get in your place through the window?" Mildred continued to press Stella for an answer.

"No, everything was secure. I don't feel safe here anymore." With that remark, Stella retreated to her apartment, leaving Mildred looking confused by the last few days of turmoil in their building.

Mildred entered her apartment and found Charlie resting in his bed; head drooped over the edge with eyes closed. The sound of the slamming door triggered a slight shift, but he remained in his doggy couch.

Mildred eyed him suspiciously, and remarked, "What have you been up to?" Unresponsive to her remark, he remained immobile, obviously exhausted by some form of physical activity.

Stella gave notice, and a month later moved out, choosing to live with her sister upstate. Mildred helped her pack. It was during that time, she slipped the roll of bills into one of Stella's moving boxes; certain she was the source of her unexpected windfall, and clearing her conscience in the process.

It wasn't long after her apartment was rented, this time by a young couple, Ron and Patti. They stayed pretty much to themselves, working by day, and traveling somewhere on weekends. Mildred met them a few times, once when they moved in, and only a couple of times after that. The first encounter was anything but pleasant.

Mildred introduced herself to her new neighbors as they were in the process of moving in. She was coming back from a walk when they met on the front sidewalk.

"Hi, you must be the new folks moving into Stella's old place?" While extending her hand in greeting she said, "My name is Mildred Peterson, and this is Charlie."

The young man was unresponsive to her gesture of friendship, but the woman graciously accepted saying, "I'm Patti, and this is my boyfriend Ron. Nice to meet you."

Ron forced a smile in return. "When we rented the apartment the landlord didn't say anything about having a dog as a neighbor. I hope he isn't a night yapper?" he asked in an unfriendly tone.

Mildred responded, but visibly hurt by his ill manners, "No. He is a good little boy, and barely makes a peep." Eager to leave after the awkward introduction, she excused herself, "Well, I see you two are busy moving in. I'll be on my way, and it was nice meeting you."

Once inside her place she unfastened the clip from the dog's collar, and said, "What a rude young man. I don't think I will like him."

Other than that, she knew very little about them until the night of the murder.

***

On Saturday morning, while Mildred prepared herself for her morning walk with Charlie, there was a knock on the door. She opened it and was met by two officers, and a man in a business suit.

"Good morning, ma'am," the man in the suit began. "I am Detective Rick Kane," he flashed his badge, but too quickly for Mildred to verify the authenticity. "We're sorry to inform you that one of your neighbors has met with an unfortunate accident."

Clearly stunned by the news she asked, "Oh no! What happened?"

"Well, it appears that the young man, who lived across the hall from you, was electrocuted by a floor fan in his bathroom. Did you ever hear or see any type of arguments between your neighbors?"

"If he had an accident, why are you asking me if they fought?"

"These questions are routine, and we always look at all the possibilities in a suspicious death," the investigator said.

"What was suspicious about his death?" Mildred inquired.

"His girlfriend claims she saw some kind of animal scampering in the shadows. It was shortly after that, he cried out, and hit the floor. We found no evidence of any animal, but the electrical cord that was connected to the fan was tampered with. An animal could have done the slivering of the cord, exposing of the wire to the wet ground. Under the circumstances, there is nothing that supports her story. Do you own any type of animal, Mrs. ah—?" prodding her for a name.

"Oh, I am sorry," she said, breaking her obvious focus on hearing the disturbing news. "My name is Mildred Peterson, and yes, I do own a small dog. But you surely don't think my little guy did anything like that? He was with me the entire evening, and morning. We were about to leave for our morning walk when you knocked on my door," she said defensively. From behind the trio of officers, Mildred saw the body being removed from her neighbor's apartment. The policemen moved a bit closer to Mildred, allowing the gurney to pass behind them, and down the stairs.

"No, Mrs. Peterson. These are routine questions. I won't keep you from your walk," the detective said, adding, "Have a nice day."

Mildred returned to her apartment, threw on a light coat, and retrieved Charlie. As she attached the leash's clip to his collar, she caught sight of some debris in his bed. A few pieces of, what appeared to be brown electrical cord insulation, lay scattered on top of the cushion. She grabbed a piece, grasping it between her thumb, and index finger, and squeezed; it was pliable under pressure.

She said nothing. Curious onlookers surrounded her as she led her dog outside. Someone in the crowd asked, "What happened?" She remained mute and stared straight ahead, letting the dog pull her along. Her stoic expression indicated she was miles away and deep in thought.

After she returned home she did not engage in the usual one-sided banter with her new puppy. In fact, she acted indifferently to his presence. His little yelps were ignored. She retired to her bedroom, and closed the door.

Once behind the security of her door she went to the nightstand and retrieved the telephone directory. Finding the listing for the local newspaper, she talked with the classified department and placed an ad.

"For Sale, puppy under a year old, purebred tan male

Puggle not fixed, has all shots $500 (212) 555-9951"

***

The landlord led Detective Kane into Mildred Peterson's apartment. An untethered puppy began to stir from his bed. Several piles of excrement littered the floor. He slowly approached the two men with his head downcast. Kane reached out, and lightly petted him with his latex gloved hand, the other hand securely holding a kerchief over his mouth.

It was only four days ago since he was in this building last, and investigating a possible homicide. The kitchen was weakly lit, the blinds, and drapes closed off the day's sunshine. A sweet sickening smell permeated the interior.

"Mildred is a person of routine, Detective. When two days' worth of newspapers remained unclaimed at her door, I became concerned." His muffled words were barely audible though the cloth cupped over his mouth. "I knocked several times. After waiting a bit, I let myself in. That is when I found her in the bedroom. I didn't touch anything," the landlord said, raising both hands into the air as if to symbolically show the policeman he was innocent of any crime. He quickly covered his mouth again as they approached the bedroom.

After examining Mildred's bloated body, the inspector retreated to the hallway, and took the landlord's statement.

Using his cellphone, he called in the death. After, he made another direct call to the crime lab's forensic pathologist.

"Stu, this is Rick Kane. When you get the Mildred Peterson case give it special attention. There are a number of strange things about this one that makes me suspicious. I think it's more than an old lady dying in her sleep. There was no visible forced entry, yet she appears to have died by suffocation."

His next call was to the animal shelter. "This is Detective Rick Kane. I have a deceased woman who owned a small dog; I'm not sure what breed. Could you send one of your vans to pick him up? I'll be here for a while with the CSI team. Okay, thanks," he clicked off the phone, and went inside Mildred's apartment to fetch the dog.

"So, what's going to happen to this dog?" Detective Kane asked the female driver of the animal rescue van.

"Usually family members, if they have any, won't take the pet. We then put them up for adoption. If no one adopts him, we'll have to put him down," she said while holding him in her arms, and scratching under his chin. "But, I don't see this little fella staying with us too long."

"By the way," Detective Kane began, "what kind of dog is this anyway?"

"This little fella is a puggle. They are a very lovable and loyal breed of dog. It's a mix between a beagle and pug." She paused, outwardly forming a bond with Charlie, and added, "Why, I may adopt this one myself. I hope my boyfriend doesn't get jealous?" she quipped, while a mischievous smile grew on her face.

ITCHY WISHY TWITCHY

He wasn't an ugly kid, but he wasn't what you could call good looking either. He was just an ordinary kid who was tormented mercilessly by his older sister, and her equally terrible friends. Freddy Freelander, so named, because his parents thought the name had a nice ring to it. And for that very reason, was the brunt of mockery simply because his name had a nice ring to it.

"Here comes Freaky Freddy Freelander, "was the usual exclamation upon his approach, or simply, "Here comes Freaky Freddy."

His awful labeling was thanks to his sister Beth, who had no use for a little brother, having enjoyed *queen* status for several years before his birth. Once she uttered her first insult to him in public, it went viral. Of course this tagging did nothing for his ego. He tended to keep a low profile, using his chameleon ability to match the paint of the closest wall. His selection of clothing, when given an opportunity, remained neutral.

Beth's insults, toward her brother, were never within earshot of their parents, knowing her words would bring instant condemnation. If Beth entertained her friends at home, without parental observation, Freddy would have to run the gauntlet of insults during the passage to his room.

"Shields up!" he yelled after entering his bedroom, the door becoming a deflector device of his own creation.

His room was a safe haven. Escape from his sister, and other tormentors were as close as the wormhole of his own creation—instantly transporting him beyond their malicious grasp. Images of spaceships, extraterrestrial beings, and alien worlds filled the confines of his chamber. He was now a billion miles away. Meanwhile, back on Earth, Fred's sister could not let matters be.

"Hey, Halloween is coming soon. Maybe we could scare the crap out of my brother," Beth said, beaming with the possibilities of terrorizing him.

Both Jan and Pat eagerly accepted the challenge, their faces contorting into a devilish appearance at the prospect of frightening Freddy. They were members of Beth's posse, and as such enjoyed celebrity status in school. They visualized themselves as an indestructible trio, lording over the sophomore class. To those outside their clique of arrogance, they were *The Three Bitches.*

"What should we wear?" asked Pat, looking toward Beth for guidance.

"Well, there are three of us. Either we go as the three blind mice, which is not at all scary, or the three witches from Macbeth."

"Witches! Yes!" cried Pat, with delight.

"Yes!" echoed Jan.

"You know, Halloween night is also the sophomore costume dance," Beth said, as she began to formulate her plan. "We can all meet here, and get dressed. Freddy will be out trick-or-treating early. My parents will also be going to a party that night, too. They do that every Halloween. After they go we will wait a bit, and terrify him when he comes home."

There were smiles all around indicating unanimous consent. Remembering the lines from Shakespeare's Hamlet, they all recited in unison, "Double, double, toil and trouble; fire burn, and caldron bubble."

The resulting laughter was so loud, even Freddy heard the hilarity from below, and wondered what could be so funny.

Freddy reclined on his bed, and robotically searched his iPod, his face mirroring each hue from the screen as he navigated with his thumbs. He liked his sister. No, not the evil side, but only the fact that he had an older sister. He only wished she could see his appreciation.

Once when he was feeling down he asked his mother if Beth liked him. Her answer was quick and encouraging.

"Beth is at that stage in her life where you remind her of the kid she once was. She just wants to appear grown-up to her friends. She'll change."

While flipping through Internet pages about *Love*, he thought about his mother's words, and an intriguing banner caught his attention. *Free Love Spells and Magic Spells* dropped into view, and begged further investigation.

His fingers immediately clicked open the invitation to examine what may be an answer to his sister troubles. A warning notice emerged, "Caution! You must be at least 18 years old to enter." His actual age of 12 did not prevent him from answering *yes*, and continued through the portal.

A flood of subjects populated the page. As he steered his way through the maze of choices he found what he was looking for. Under *Love*, he located ten choices, but only one glimmered of a solution—*Making Someone Like You*. Another click and a spell of incredible simplicity filled the screen.

"Itchy Wishy Twitchy"

Say me three times

Under a full moon,

While your clock thrice chimes,

But under evening's gloom.

Then add the name of person wicked,

Persuading a change to the afflicted.

Some say there is no such thing as a coincidence, but the next full moon was less than two weeks away—on Halloween. Freddy saw nothing bad in the spell. He wanted to make his sister like him, nothing more.

Halloween arrived, and as planned, Beth's friends joined her in transforming themselves into witches. Her parents already were gone, but she had been given strict instructions about the evening before they left.

"Beth," her mother began. "Be nice to Freddy. Don't tease him, and make sure you get home by eleven o'clock. No sleepover tonight either. Tomorrow is Friday, and you have school. Trick-or-treating ends tonight by six because of sunset. The city doesn't want little kids running around after dark, so you will have to hand out the candy. You can go to your dance after that. Okay?"

Beth dutifully replied she would, and wished them a good time at their party. A devilish smile emerged from her innocent-looking face, once the front door closed on her departing parents. Her schedule did not conform to the wishes of her mother; so a little modification was in order.

Freddy was out trick-or-treating. He had disguised himself as a ghost. The costume served two purposes; one, it was easy to make, and two, no one would know who he was, thus freeing him from bullying.

Beth, Pat, and Jan occupied their time dressing, applying makeup, and talking trash about fellow classmates.

"So I said to that creepy Marlow," Beth declared, "'You talk about it. We live it.'"

All three of them burst into laughter, accented with a couple of witch-cackle noises.

"We'll get you, Marlow, and your little dog too!" proclaimed Jan with a menacing tone. Further hilarity followed. The sound of the doorbell broke the mood.

"It's no big deal, just kids wanting to fill their fat faces with candy. Be quiet, they'll go away," said Beth.

"Won't your mother wonder why you have all that candy left?" Pat asked.

"I'll just hide it in my dresser. She won't even know."

The three girls finished converting their outer selves into the accurate version of themselves. With wart-spotted noses, greenish complexions furrowed with mascara, deep shadowed eyes, and blood-red lipstick, they became the distillation of wickedness. When finished, they laughed in approval. The doorbell rang again, and again it was ignored.

"Freddy, will be home pretty soon," Beth reminded her wicked sisters. "Let's get ready. He'll have to go through the hallway on his way upstairs. As soon as we see him come up the walkway, Jan, you hide in the hall closet. Pat, you can lie in wait on the other side of the basement door, and I will stay inside my room. When I dash out of my room you two will come out of your hiding places."

They all agreed. After going into the front room, they perched themselves in a kneeling position on the couch, the back of which faced the street. Like three jackals waiting on prey, their black fingernails curled around the rear cushion while they gossiped.

"So I asked Marlow, 'What are you going to be for Halloween?'" Beth began. "She then tells me, 'Give your mouth, and legs a break, and shut them for once,' then storms off."

"So what did you say or—," Pat began to ask, but was cut short by the appearance of Freddy approaching the house.

"Hurry! Everyone hide!" Beth commanded. They all scatted to their designated hiding spots.

Using his key, Freddy opened the front door, unsuspecting of the trap. After turning on a light in the living room he went to the refrigerator, and grabbed a can of soda. With his bag of candy loot, and unopened drink in hand, he began to walk through the hallway. As he passed Beth's room she sprang from its darkness, frightening him into dropping everything, soda included.

That was Pat, and Jan's cue to materialize from the shadows. They joined Beth in dancing around a terrified Freddy, who remained frozen. He covered his eyes, and cowered under the torments of the three while they had their fun. With cackles, and demonic laughter they bolted from the house emerging like banshees. Screeching, and laughing they ran down the sidewalk on the way to the school's Halloween dance.

Freddy picked himself up, and surveyed the floor. Candy was strewn about, some deformed or broken under the weight of witches' feet. He gathered the candy, and dented soda can, went up the stairs, and crashed onto his bed. The final abuse followed when he opened his soda, and its contents exploded onto his face.

After eating some of candy, and washing it down with the remaining soda, he retrieved the spell. *This will be the night*, he thought.

Beth arrived a half-hour beyond the directed curfew, but neither of her parents was home. She had a good time at the dance; in fact it was a great time. She even had an opportunity to trip Marlow, who was carrying two cups of punch, sending her headfirst into a bunch of boys. Marlow's Snow White's dress became soaked with pink punch, and she had to leave early.

A slight smile came across Beth's face as she kicked off her shoes, and fell backward onto the bed. The events of the day proved exhausting, and she felt blameless knowing everyone got what was due. Laying there in triumph she succumbed to sleep, which descended on her without warning.

***

Freddy set his alarm for two-thirty, which allowed plenty of time to dress, and get into position. He retrieved the spell, and threw on a jacket over his pajamas. The house was silent as he carefully crept down the stairway in his sock-covered feet. He paused in the living room, taking note of the time on the grandfather clock—he had fifteen minutes to go.

He slowly slid the back patio door open, just enough for him to squeeze outside, and onto the wood deck. The moon was full. A few wisps of clouds stroked its face, but it was bright enough to read by. The unfolding of the incantation made a sound Freddy was certain would alert everyone in the house. His heart was pounding. He waited.

The first strike of the clock's chime sent him into action. "Itchy Wishy Twitchy," almost surprising himself by the resonance in his voice. "Itchy Wishy Twitchy," he blurted again on the second strike. "Itchy Wishy Twitchy—Beth," he uttered in closing. The evening air quickly became noiseless.

Freddy remained under the moon's glow for a while, expecting something to happen. He was looking for a sign, a little hint that his effort was a success. None came, and after a few minutes he retraced his steps upstairs, and went back to sleep.

***

The scream was terrifying, and everyone in the house stirred to life. Doors flung open and banged against walls. The sound of footsteps converged on the source—Beth standing outside her room dripping wet, and wrapped in a white robe. Her face was green with furrowed lines. Her deep-set eyes darted from side to side as she pleaded to her parents for a solution.

"What's wrong with me? It won't come off! I look hideous. I can't go to school looking like this," she stammered.

"I'm sure we can get that makeup off," reassured her mother. "Come, let's get back in your bathroom, and let me have a look." Grabbing Beth by the hand they moved inside.

"Perhaps some paint thinner would help?" offered Beth's father. His suggestion only brought more tears, and an inaudible response from Beth.

Freddy followed his regular morning routine. After a breakfast of orange juice, and cereal he left for school, happy to leave the chaos behind. He did wonder if he had anything to do with what happened to Beth. *It wasn't a bad spell*, he thought.

After school he cautiously walked past Beth's room on his way upstairs. He could hear his mother talking with her. "We have an appointment with Doctor Connors on Monday. He will have a look, and see what has to be done." Her words were not reassuring based on the wail coming from Beth.

At dinner time only three of them surrounded the table. "Beth will not be eating with us tonight," Freddy's mother explained. "She isn't feeling well."

"What's wrong with her, Mom?" asked Freddy.

"She has some kind of skin condition. I will be taking her to see Doctor Connors next week."

"Freddy, I called the school, and told them she was ill. Would you please pick up her class assignments on your way past her school on Monday?"

"Sure, Mom," Freddy replied. "What classroom do I go to?"

"Go to the principal's office on the first floor. Someone will tell you where it is. And thanks Freddy; you are doing a nice thing for her."

***

On Monday he did as his mother asked. Before going to his room he knocked on Beth's bedroom door. He hadn't seen her the entire weekend, so he wasn't sure of her mood.

"Who's there?" yelled Beth.

"It's Fred. I have your homework, Mom told me to get for you."

"Come in, and don't you say a thing. Got that?" Beth demanded.

"Yes," he fearfully answered through the closed door.

When he did open the door he saw Beth sitting cross-legged on the edge of her bed. A sickly-looking green hue covered all her exposed skin, her white robe magnifying the contrast. He was stunned by her appearance, and was unable to ask her anything for fear his question would only produce a torrent of name-calling. He simply handed her the assignments, and turned back to the door.

"Thank you," she said in a low voice, barely audible, but it brought a smile to Freddy's face as he closed the door behind him.

***

The doctors were unable to determine the cause of the complexion change in Beth, and her apparent accelerated aging. She became a recluse, never leaving the house except for medical reasons. When their parents passed away, the house was willed to Beth, and Freddy.

Freddy Freelander ultimately got married, and he let Beth have his portion of the house. Fred, as he was known among his friends, became a successful businessman as well as a great humanitarian. Having tended for his sister all those years, made him a caring person, and well-loved in the community. But most of all, his sister loved him the best.

EVERY CURIOUS MAN AND CAT

I'm sitting in my office having a conversation with my friend Jack, Jack Daniel's to be exact. But he is doing all the talking. The night is hot, the kind of heat that sticks to your skivvies. The noise from the city below is fighting with the fan that clatters on top of the filing cabinet. Sweeping the room with the August night air, it stirs the papers on my desk, held in place with a deck of Luckies. I've got a choice—keep filing or keep talking with Jack. Jack is winning.

There's a knock on my door. Anyone walking three flights of stairs on a hot August night is either trouble, or took a very wrong turn to get to the subway. Only a single shape moves across the frosted glass.

"Door's open," I yell, removing my sleeping legs off the top of my desk, and reaching inside the top desk drawer. My hand is resting on my Colt Police Positive Special. I'm not taking chances, because I didn't have change for the subway.

The door slowly swings in and a dame in a tan trench coat stands in the opening. Her face is not visible because the light from the corridor silhouettes her. I can tell she's about five-ten, the hallway's glow highlighting her blonde hair. Her right hand is in the pocket of the coat, while her left hand rests on a purse slung over her shoulder.

"Rick Ralls?"

"You asking me, or you just showing me ya know how to read?"

Without waiting for an invitation she steps in and closes the door behind her. She starts to remove her hand from the coat pocket.

"Hold on, sister. Nice and easy, tip your mitt slowly," I say, sliding my trigger finger inside the Colt's guard, but keeping it hidden in the drawer. I give her the up-and-down, waiting to see the next act.

She removes her hand, and exposes both of them, palms out, toward me.

"You mind if I take off this coat? I'm warm, I was expecting rain today."

I give her a quick nod. After untying the front belt, she tosses back the coat, revealing a couple of nice pillows that would make Mae West jealous. Her black dress is more suited to ballroom dancing than climbing stairs at night. By the size of the rocks around her neck, I figure this dame has moolah, or knows someone who does.

"What can I do for you, doll?" I ask, thinking I may have finally hit pay dirt by the glare coming off her necklace.

"I'm looking for someone. He has something that belongs to me. I want it back."

"Okay," I say, "If this person has something that belongs to you, why don't you go to the cops?"

"It isn't that simple. The police would ask too many questions."

"Yah, I try to stay away from the clubhouse myself," I say, studying her and trying to figure if this dame is playing me. "Why me, lady?"

"I'm running out of time, and your light was on," she says, coyly smiling at my question.

"I will need a mug shot, a down payment, and a way to find you."

She opens her purse, reaches in and pulls out a fist full of cabbage, enough to choke a horse. "I think this should handle the down payment?"

She places three banded stacks of century notes on my desk, and asks, "Do we have a deal?" Before I can answer she adds, "You get the other half when I get my property."

That's enough sugar to keep me in Jack Daniel's the rest of my life, I'm thinking. Why, with sixty thousand Simoleons, I can leave this crappy town and take a powder to Miami.

"You got it, sister," I say. "Now all I need is a photo and what I have to snatch."

"Here is the snapshot," she says, and places the picture on top the stack of bills. His puss looks like a pushover with his moon face, big ears, and a puckered yap.

"He looks like a daisy. What's the prize?" I ask, expecting a big-time heist, considering the stack of C-notes on my desk.

"I want a gun he stole from me." She drops that on me like someone asking to pass the salt for her eggs.

"Hold on, sister. I don't mind laying down a little muscle, but I don't want to bop someone, and lose my shamus ticket, or get a lift to the hoosegow. You expecting me to scatter some lead?"

"I don't think you'll need your gun, if you have the element of surprise on your side. He won't be expecting you because he doesn't know you. It'll be easy."

"If it's easy as pie, why don't you do it yourself, sister?"

"Like I said, Mister Ralls, he knows me. I don't think I can get within a hundred yards before he would spot me."

"This fella have a name?" I ask, thinking more of the dough than good sense.

"He goes by the name of Billy Bee, and hangs around the docks at a place called Monternoe's Bar and Grille."

"That his real name, 'Billy Bee'?"

"Don't know for sure. That's what he likes to be called. All I know is that he has something of mine."

"That's a lot of scratch for a roscoe. You can buy yourself a whole army for that kind of dough."

She gives me this wounded look, and says, "It has sentimental value."

"That's a lot of schmaltziness," I quip. "One last thing, I need a number to drop a dime on when the deed is done."

Without answering, she gets up, drapes her coat over her left arm, hiding her purse under its fold, and heads for the door. Stopping, she turns toward me, and says, "Like I found you tonight, I will find you again, so you can add that dime to your profits."

"Okay, got it, but what's your name, doll?"

"The name's Violet."

With that, she opens the door, disappearing into the hall, leaving me alone with my friend Jack. I take a gasper out of the deck of Luckies, light up, prop my number elevens on my desk, and think of Miami in winter.

***

I sleep in the next day. For breakfast I go down the street from my apartment to a little hash house called Curlies'. I wash down my meal of bacon and eggs with a cup of java, and give the waitress a big tip because I'm in a good mood. Since this job had an element of risk, I'm also packing iron. I'm not looking for trouble; I just want to be ready when it finds me.

I hail a hack, and we head down to the river. The cabbie wants to talk my ear off, but I tell him to can the chatter, "I had a bad ice cube last night." He lets me alone until we arrive at the docks.

"Well mister, this is it, Monternoe's. That'll be ninety-five cents," he says, while holding out his hand. I give him a fin and tell him to "keep the change." Seeing the size of the tip he springs out of the driver's side and opens my door.

As I step out onto the sidewalk, the smell of the river, mixed with the exhaust of the passing traffic, made me wonder why I stay in this crummy town. I give the place the onceover and walk toward the entrance. A Schlitz beer sign flashing its neon light in the front window, enticing customers to quench their thirst inside. I didn't need any invitation.

The place is long and narrow; the back bar mirror is covered with shelves stacked to the ceiling with bottles of hooch. This is my kind-of-place. Five people sat at wide gaps along the mahogany bar; a boob being conned by a broad, a bruno studying his half empty glass of beer, and a jasper that looks like an easy mark. I walk through the blue haze of smoke toward the bartender, who is gumming with patron five, a gink whose breezer is as red as Rudolf's.

The barkeep stops his yacking and moves toward me. "What'll it be, mister?"

I lay down the picture of Billy Bee, and ask, "You know this guy?"

"Who wants to know?"

"He just inherited a lot of money from his uncle in Poughkeepsie, and I'm here to see that he gets it."

"Funny, you don't look like a shyster. Why do you think you'll find him here?"

After laying out a double sawbuck on the bar, I say, "Here, maybe you can get a pair of glasses and improve your vision?"

He looks at the bill, pulls it toward himself, and says, "As a matter of fact he does look familiar. I think I saw him here once or twice. Does his late uncle have a lot of money for his favorite nephew?"

I want to wrap this job up fast, so I slid another twenty at him, saying, "His name is Billy Bee."

"Oh, yeah, now I remember. He comes in here at night, does a little hustlin' on the pool table, has a few drinks, and leaves. No trouble, ever."

"Thanks, and let's keep this our secret. I want to surprise him. Okay?" I say, eyeing him skeptically.

"You bet, mister."

I say in parting, "See you around. Hope you like those new glasses?" He smiles, flicks the glass drying cloth over his shoulder and walks back to the gink.

Taking the air I look for a phone booth to call me a cab. Finding one, it stinks like a john, so I got on the horn and scram out. Lighting a stick, I wait for my ride to the office.

My office is tight as Tut's tomb, so I open the window and turn on the fan. I take my jacket off and lay down on the couch to give my dogs a break. I want to be rested for tonight's job, so a short trip to dreamland is in order.

***

The sound of a siren broke my siesta. I walk to the sink, splash water on my puss and use some Daniel's to rinse my mouth, because I'm out of Listerine. After gliding my Colt into my shoulder holster, I put on my coat in spite of the heat.

Traffic is light on my way to Monternoe's, and the cabbie isn't the talkative type, so I'm able to imagine what life's about in Miami. I give the hack driver a fin, but the goose barely moves. So much for being a nice guy.

This time the joint is packed like the five o'clock subway to Queens. There were three stick-men pulling the brew, my earlier bird must have been at the ophthalmologist getting fitted for glasses.

I push my way to the back, found a seat with a view of the pool table. Billy Bee looks better in his mug shot. His alderman's pot made him appear like a boozehound, although steady on his feet. He is angling a sucker on the hook. After watching his fish scratch a shot, Billy set the cue ball in the kitchen. He then feathers a shot on the eight ball and it drops. Billy's two-bit investment wins him two berries, which he scarfs up and slides into his pants' pocket. Seemingly satisfied with his night's take, he slams the rest of his beer down his gullet, and starts for the door.

"Billy Bee!" I call out, slightly above the racket in the bar.

He turns around, looks at me, and asks, "Yep, who's asking?"

"The name's Rick Ralls."

"Never heard of you, mister. Whaddya want from me?"

"Violet sent me to get something that belongs to her. She tells me you got it," I say, pulling back my jacket just enough for him to cop a peek I'm sporting iron.

His face got as red as a stoplight, and I wasn't sure if it's the mention of Violet's name, or the gat under my arm.

"Listen, mister, err— Rick, I don't know what that broad told you, but it belongs to me," he says, and moves closer to my table. "You aren't going to pull that piece in here, there're too many people."

"Well, bub, you can't stay in here forever. Sooner or later ya gotta get some air, and I'll be waiting," I say, and push my index finger into his fat gut.

He looks straight ahead at me, like a sphinx, and asks, "Whaddya think I have that Violet says belongs to her?"

"She claims you have a gun that has sentimental meaning to her."

He starts to laugh, but cuts the jolly Saint Nick routine and tells me,

"You're on a fool's errand, Rick. You been sold a bill of goods, and you don't have a clue."

He pushes past me and melts into the bar's patrons. I start to tail him through crush of people, but by the time I hit the street he does a Houdini on me.

***

Realizing I bungled the job by showing my hand before the final draw, I take an intermission in my office, thinking of my next move. While considering my options, Violet decides to see the view from my office in daylight. This time she doesn't knock; I guess she thought she's always welcome. Well, after all, thirty grand does buy you a ticket.

This time she looks like she stepped out of a Dior photo-spread in Look magazine. She wore an undersized sleeveless red blouse, with three low buttons at the midriff struggling to keep the cleavage intact. The dress is black, hourglass shaped; cut high enough to show off her gams. Besides the clutch purse, she held a matching black jacket; I guess if she decides to stop into church.

"What brings you here so soon? Miss me already?" I ask. Before she can answer, I add, "I'm still working the case."

She gives me this unimpressed look and takes a seat, and says, "Time's running out. You gave me the impression that you can handle this quickly."

"Listen, doll, these things take time. I met Billy, but I lost him."

"You met him and you lost him, too!" she shouts. "Billy may look stupid, but he isn't. You're going to have a tough time getting a second chance now that he knows you."

Her departure is sudden. Moving for the door, she abruptly stops, turns to me and says, "I need that gun. Get it for me, now! I didn't give you that kind of money so you can sit in your office, and do—whatever you do." She slams the door so hard I thought my name would pop off the glass.

Something Billy Bee said made me think twice about this dame's story. It's about being 'sold a bill of goods' that stuck in my craw, and gnaw at my brain.

Grabbing my coat, I spring from my office following the telltale sound of fleeing high heels. By the time I hit the pavement she's getting into a cab. No doubt the cabbie was told to wait, and I'm sure the meter was spinning.

As her cab pulls away, I spot another one. I think she's too upset to see if she is being followed. Anyway, I hail the yellow bucket; tell the driver, "Follow that taxi."

"Okay, mister, just like in the movies," he says with a touch of mockery in his voice. "You a peeper on a case, bud?"

"Something like that, just don't lose her," I reply without looking at him, instead keeping my eyes fixed ahead.

After a while it's obvious she's traveling toward the docks and not far away from Billy's haunt. Still several blocks from Monternoe's, they stop in the middle of the street, and take a sharp left down a narrow alley. I knew if we followed we would be spotted. I tell my driver to go a bit further and pull over. I flip him a sawbuck and tell him to wait. "Sure thing, mister," he says, this time with a little more interest in the game.

It's getting dark and the streetlights aren't lit yet. Quickly crossing the street, I hug the buildings, making my way back to the alley entrance. Peeking around the corner, I spot her ducking into a doorway with the cab's lights fading away. I think, okay sister, what are you up to?

I left my piece in my office drawer, so I wasn't packing the kind of weight I would have liked. The door she went into is slightly ajar. That told me she's making this a short visit and would be back this way soon.

The building appears to be some sort of warehouse, and I'm glad that the cement floor is not going to give me away like creaking wood flooring. Anyway, I watch my step and follow the dusty trail left by her spiked heels. Her route follows along a narrow passageway that ends at a heavy, steel-framed door and with reinforced mesh over a frosted window. There's a glow of light playing on the inside pane, occasionally a shadow in flight would touch the other side.

I ease open the door just enough to get a look of the interior. What I saw defied understanding. Placed in the center of the warehouse is a tubular metal structure, about twenty feet high and maybe only eight feet wide. It looks like a giant bullet without a primer bottom or extractor groove. There's a doorway of sorts on the side, but seems to lack hinges or a doorknob.

I start to see some movement inside. Violet, whatever she did, is done, and begins to leave. Not wanting to be seen, I quickly close the door and walk back to the alley.

Once outside, I made a beeline to my waiting cab and told him to hold his position for a while. We wait for a half hour before telling my driver it's time to scram out. Maybe she noticed my footprints, or maybe she thought they were Billy Bee's, so she probably bugged out another way.

Speaking of Billy Bee, it's time to pay him another visit. But first, I need to stop at my office, and get some heat.

***

I didn't waste my time looking for Billy at Monternoe's Bar and Grille. He's not stupid enough to double act there, but he wasn't a hermit either and is probably looking for action somewhere else. I'm betting it would be between that place and Violet's warehouse. The fact that there were twelve gin mills along the way would make the job a little tough on my liver.

The tour of dive-land ends after three stops. I spot Billy performing his hustling hobby in a place called Romeos. He hadn't seen me, so I decide to wait out front. After finding a nice recessed spot across the street, I make myself comfortable and wait for the worm to leave the apple.

I didn't wait long. There is a bit of a dustup in the place and someone spits Billy into the street, saying, "Get the hell outta here. Don't think of trying to use this place as your con shop again."

Billy wobbles backwards and lands sunny side up near the curbing. Regaining his composure, and dignity, he brushes himself off, and turns to leave in the direction of the warehouse. I start to follow him, but I stay on the opposite side for a bit. When he makes a left turn down a side street I cross over and tighten the distance between us.

His walk's a bit unsteady, giving me some advantage, allowing me to surprise him from behind. "Billy, don't turn around," I say, holding my Police Special against his spine. "You move, and I'll burn powder and pump metal in your back. Got that?"

"Got it," he replies in a cowed voice.

"Now let's get into this gangway and talk," prodding him along with the business end of my revolver.

"Grab air, and turn around slowly," I say, while backing away from him. "Now you're gonna sing, and if I don't like the song, they'll be fittin' you for a Chicago overcoat. I want to know about Violet, and that tube thing."

Billy's eyes widen, "How do you know about that?"

"I know where it is, but I don't know what it is. Now spill your guts, or I'll spill them for you."

"Okay, take it easy, Rick. Here's the story, but you're not going to believe me."

"Try me."

"That tube, as you call it, is actually a time and space travel device."

"Listen, Billy, my patience is running on empty, and I don't need a cock-and-bull story. I didn't exactly get here on a turnip wagon. Start again, this time the truth."

Billy began to squirm, looking nervously at my pistol, then back at me. "I told you, you wouldn't believe me," he says.

"Let's try something different, Billy. Let me have the gun that belongs to Violet. Once I have that, we can start over again. Now reach in your pocket pull it out as slowly as grass grows."

Billy takes his right hand and slowly reaches into the inside pocket of his jacket. Just as slowly, he begins to remove it, revealing a shimmering object that did not resemble any type of gun I ever saw.

"Hand it over," I demand, while keeping an eye on Billy, for any sign of a double cross.

Once in my possession I slid the object in the left outside flap of my coat. "Now let's hear that story again."

"You're not going to like it, but once more here it is. As I said, the thing in the warehouse is a time and space travel machine. Violet, or better known in our world, Fashula, accompanied me on a trip of exploration to this world of yours. We were supposed to gather information about your civilization and return. One thing went wrong; I like it here and want to stay. Fashula—I mean, Violet, didn't. I removed the activating device, thus preventing us from leaving."

"That's quite a story, Billy. Why does Violet call it a gun?"

"It is a gun, a transmitter, and a key to the transporter. It's all of those things plus more, but too complex for me to explain to you now."

As far-fetched as the story is, I'm thinking it could hold water. "What's stopping you from just dropping the thing in her lap and taking a powder on Earth?"

"She wouldn't let me. If I gave it to her she would use the weapon function and vaporize me."

"I don't know if you're pulling my leg, but here is an idea. You just disappear; head out West or someplace other than here. I give her the gun, or whatever it is, I get paid, she goes home and we all live happy ever after. You have any money, Billy? I mean other than the money you got from hustling pool."

"Yes. When we first got here, Violet, and I found a way to earn enough to fund our exploration of your world."

"It sounds to me that everyone will be happy with that plan," I say, waiting for any objection from Billy.

"I don't think she thought you and I would be talking about this. My guess, I think she may have believed that you were going to kill me and give her the device," Billy says with some relief in his voice.

"So we got a deal?"

Billy Bee nods and adds, "I will 'head west' as you say, but before I do, I want to leave you some advice, and a word of caution."

"Go ahead," I say.

"You know where the transporter is. Remove the main module from the device I just gave you; tape it to the door of the machine. Get the money she promised you first. When you give her the gun, tell her what you did and where the missing part is. Keep your weapon handy, there is nothing she is not capable of doing. If you give her that device intact she will vaporize you; that's how ruthless she is."

"Now Mister Ralls, I think I'm going to catch a train." Billy Bee inches his way past me and onto the sidewalk. Only the sound of his departing footsteps can be heard as he melts into the night.

Yes, I thought, it's a good deal for everyone, and I'm feeling real good about my future life in Miami.

***

It's nighttime when, unlike her previous visit, Violet knocks on my door. One thing that can be said for this dame is that she's a good dresser. Her shapely figure is well accented in her indigo, Capri three-quarter pants and matching short-sleeved jacket. The collar is raised behind her neck, with the opened front plunging down halfway to the waist. For modesty, I figure, she tucked a silk ascot into the V-neck, but the whole getup is far from modest. She has some oyster fruit around her neck, and a couple pieces dangling from each ear.

I eye her ascot; my gaze then follows its line to her face. She has an impatient look.

"Well, did you get what I sent you to get?" she asks, as she makes her way towards my desk. She's holding a black clutch purse. It's big enough to hold some heat, or thirty Gs', but not both. She sits down, and waits for me to answer.

Her package is inside my top drawer. I pull the drawer open, and bring it to full view on top of the desk with my left hand; the other hand rests on my Colt. Her eyes brighten like a lighthouse beam on a dark night.

"I kept my end of the deal, now the cash sister."

She reaches in her purse, while I tighten my grip on my cannon. Without much fanfare, she smacks the stack of bills next to the prize, and grabs for it . After picking it up her smile fades, and says, "Something missing. It looks like you removed the main part; the part that makes it work."

"Yea, that's my insurance doll. I had a talk with Billy before I muscled the gun from him. Seems that object can do all sorts of things, including toasting me. So I took his advice, and removed the shells from this bean-shooter so you wouldn't get tempted.

"Seems Billy likes it here, and decided to take the air, leaving you to drive home solo. He's on a rattler heading west by now. So you got what you wanted, and I see by the stack of green, I got what I wanted."

"Where's the missing part?" By the tone in her voice she's none too happy.

"Don't worry doll, I know where your vehicle is parked. You don't think I hang around this office all day long, do ya? I hid the missing chunk over the transom leading into the warehouse. It's yours for the taking." I didn't follow Billy's suggestion to tape it to the contraption; on the chance it would be a double-cross.

"Well mister Ralls, it would appear you have outsmarted me, but we both got what we wanted. Didn't we, Rick?"

"I guess so, doll-face," grinning my satisfaction and feeling a sense of accomplishment. She gets up, leaves my office and out of my life.

***

I'm recuperating beachside at the Fontainebleau after a night at the Latin Quarter, the girls were plentiful, but their costumes weren't. The Miami climate certainly agrees with me. I should have left New York years ago. The only thing I'm working on now is my tan and second Singapore Sling. Everything here is glamour, glamour with a capital G and I'm taking it all in.

"Would you care for a newspaper sir, and may I refresh your drink?" the beach waitress asks. Who am I to keep a girl from making a living, so I say yes to both offers and hand her a sawbuck? She gives me the paper and takes off for my drink.

I open the Miami News; check the bangtail section, and the daily races. I look for a nag with the right sounding name, never believing the forecasters, I'm a hunch man. Seeing nothing that caught my interest, I start to flip through the pages, looking for anything to spark my curiosity.

Well, near the back, under the fold I spot something that certainly made my eyes pop their sockets. A small news box from Las Vegas sent a chill down my spine, even though it's ninety degrees outside. "MAN IGNITES WHILE SLEEPING. Las Vegas, Nevada – A man, only known as Billy Bee, burst into flame, apparently through spontaneous combustion. The Clark County Coroner could give no other explanation for this rare phenomenon, as the room was locked from the inside and there was no evidence of any foul play."

"That poor son-of-a-bitch. He should have changed his name," I say out loud.

My attention is fixed to the newspaper story when the sun is blocked by a couple of guys that turn out to be johns. Looking through my cheaters, they were wearing cheap 'Monkey Ward' off-the-rack suits, thin-rimed fedoras, with multicolor striped ribbon banding, which didn't match the suits.

"You Rick Ralls?" one of them asks.

"Depends who's asking."

"I am Special Agent Malone, and this is Special Agent Burrows, we're from the FBI. We are placing you under arrest for the robbery of the Hammer & Hopkins Bank." The one doing the talking flashes his shield while the other pulls out a pair of cuffs.

"Mister Ralls, put on your robe, we're taking you to our Miami office," says the one with the bracelets.

I comply, holding out my hands after I secure my robe. The agent drapes The Miami News over my hands to conceal the cuffs and we start to leave. Just then the waitress returns with my drink. "Your drink sir," she calls out.

"Hold it doll, I'll be back in ten," not explaining the year part of the ten, the usual bit for a bank heist.

So, the dame turns out to be one smart cookie after all. I should've figured that her cash wasn't earned from working at the White Castle, after getting wind this babe was literally out of this world. Billy gets fried, and I end up doing only a nickel for good behavior in the slammer, for something I didn't do, with Violet doing a solo somewhere among the stars. Sure, I could have spilled my guts and leveled with the Feds, but the nuthouse wasn't my cup of tea either. I probably shouldn't have answered the door to my office in the first place.

A BEAR ATE MY SISTER

Thank you for coming. I wasn't sure you would, considering the circumstances. I'm sorry I can't offer you anything to drink, but please, take a seat. I will tell you everything.

My sister and I left school at the usual time and began to walk home. Because she was younger than me, it was my duty to escort her. I didn't mind at first, but she was much slower and I was usually in a hurry. My task became more unpleasant, and I more unwilling, as time went on.

One day, the day of the tragedy, I eagerly wanted to work on a science project for school, so we took a shortcut through the woods. My sister protested because she knew our parents strictly forbad us to go into the forest. I told her it was all right this time.

It took some coaxing to convince her. I actually had to pull her along a bit when we first began. After promising a treat of some candy, when we got home, she moved more willingly. We entered the woods near the old windmill. You must know the place, just east of Willow's Crossing.

The sun was low on the horizon, but I knew we could get through the forest before dark, if we hurried. Using it as a beacon, I set a course for its orange light, while it occasionally played hide-and-seek behind the trees we were advancing on. My sister said she was scared. I told her there was nothing to fear.

We had traveled about halfway through a heavy section of thicket when my sister said she heard a strange sound. She thought it came from behind us. I told her it was probably nothing, but to be safe she should walk in front of me. My sister agreed and I followed within an arm's length of her.

Suddenly she stopped, quickly turned toward me and exclaimed that she heard the sound again. Her mood changed from fear to panic. She started to scream. She raised her arms to shield her from what she saw. My own body became warm and I felt the hot breath of something nearby. I was afraid to turn around.

Soon an unknown creature pressed against my back, pushing me into her trembling body. I was helpless and did all I could to protect my sister from its advance. I thought if I remained between the beast and my sister I could shield her from its murderous claws. I was wrong.

Its breath became more feverish as its piercing claws slashed at her flesh. Her screams intensified as her blood spattered onto me. My arms violently waved in the air in an effort to thwart the creature's probing nails. Abruptly her cries ceased and her limp body collapsed at my feet. The monster, having killed my sister, fled into the shadowy forest. The warmth from my sister's blood on me diminished rapidly and I grew cold.

I became terrified. I was now alone. I wondered, how was I going to tell our—I mean, my parents my sister was killed? With barely a sliver of light left as my guide out of the woods, I hastened to break the news.

When my parents saw me covered in blood they became anxious and wanted to know what happened to my sister. Actually they became hysterical. I told them a bear ate her and I did everything I could to save her. They didn't believe me. No one believed me.

I suppose you won't believe me either. You know you're not the first newspaper reporter to ask me about my sister. Years ago I had more company. Actually, I had as many as two a week, and not only reporters either.

You're going? Well, thank you for visiting me. I really appreciate the company. When you tell your story, try to convince them it really was a bear that ate my sister. Goodbye—someone will let you out.

THE THAUMATROPE

Professor Billings sat with his chair facing the window, watching the rising sun push the shadows across the campus grounds. He thought of the implications of his discovery and like all great achievements, he wondered about the ramifications for future generations. The findings prompted his early arrival, as he eagerly wanted to work on the final draft, certain his paper would earn him a Nobel Peace Prize.

Deep in contemplation, his focus was abruptly interrupted when his secretary tapped on the door and poked her head into the room.

"Good morning professor," she began with a tone of hesitation in her voice. While remaining hidden behind the door, except for her face, she said, "I wasn't certain you were here. There is a Mr. Phillips who wishes to see you. I don't have him on your schedule. Do you want me to send him away?"

When the silence of his room was broken by her entry he instinctively swiveled his chair in her direction.

"Did he say what he wanted?" he inquired.

"No, but he told me to say "Thaumatrope" if you were to ask," she said. Her own face proclaimed a look of puzzlement.

Professor Billings' looked stunned. He sat upright and leaned forward on his desk, both arms covering several papers haphazardly scattered over his large desk calendar.

His normal, self-assured demeanor suddenly faded. "Yes, yes. Send him in," he responded. Rising to his feet he hastily gathered the papers before him, throwing the mass of paperwork into the center top drawer.

Professor Billings' secretary, Miss Hass, returned with Mr. Phillips in tow, holding the door for him she asked, "Will you be needing anything else professor?"

While looking at his caller he invited, "Would you care for a cup of coffee Mr. Phillips?"

Waving his hand in the air in rejection of the offer, he said, "No thanks." Professor Billings extended a hand over his desk in welcoming. Mr. Phillips accepted and seated himself in one of the two chairs opposite the professor, without an invitation to do so.

Mr. Phillips appeared to be in his mid-fifties, chiseled featured, tall and thinly built. He wore a white dress shirt, a three-button black Worsted wool suit, impeccably tailored and his black wingtip shoes were brightly polished. Everything about him was faultless. Even his symmetrical double Windsor knotted silk gray tie had a perfectly centered dimple.

After quickly sizing up his unscheduled visitor, Professor Billings spoke. "What can I do for you today, and why did you announce yourself with the word "thaumatrope?"

"I knew that word would get your attention. You used it only once during one of your lectures about two years ago. It was during the presentation you speculated on the possibility of stopping the apparent movement of atoms. Your off-the-cuff idea about the persistence of vision developed into a theory of atomic suspension. As you began to explore the possibilities you realized the achievement lay within your grasp. All public pronouncements ceased and you continued your work in secret.

Professor Thomas Billings sat staring at his guest and the disclosure, hesitant to say anything. Eventually he asked, "How do you know all this?"

"The government takes an interest in the functions of the universities. When a new political idea or scientific breakthrough of note comes to light, it investigates. In your case, we followed your work and knew you were going to publish soon."

"How could you know, only my secretary and myself handled the transcripts?" Billings asked skeptically.

"Anything handled electronically leaves a trail. Frankly, as a man of science, you should know this more than the average individual."

"Okay, so now you know. Why are you here?" Having recovered from the surprise revelation, the professor spoke in more of a challenging tone.

Mr. Phillips shifted in his seat and placed both hands on his lap, one resting on the other. He began, "I have been sent here to ask you not to publish your work – at least not yet. The government believes your discovery could have potential ramifications to national security. Your find is beyond the financial capabilities of this university to pursue further research or development. Because of this limit, your administrators would solicit assistance from the federal government. When it did, it would become public and we would not like the publicity."

As Mr. Phillips talked Billings' face flushed with rage realizing the repercussions to his findings. "Neither you or the federal government is going to stop the publishing of my discoveries," the professor fumed. "I will not be cheated from my award!" he exclaimed, boldly rising to his feet in open defiance to the proposal.

Phillips remained seated, unaffected by the open hostility. "Please, professor, sit down," he calmly responded. Raising both hands in a calming gesture, waving them downward, indicating he wanted Billings to sit down. Reluctantly he obliged his request.

For a brief moment neither man spoke. Mr. Phillips sat looking straight and erect in a Sphinx-like pose, both arms reposing on the chair's armrests. The silence was rigid. Slowly Phillips eased into the strain and calmly spoke, "I want to assure you professor that no one is trying to steal anything from you; your discovery is yours. We want you to continue working on your project. In fact, your budget will be limitless and you will have complete control."

Professor Billings leaned back in his chair, apparently comforted by the proposal. "Will I continue to work here at the university?" His demeanor somewhat recovered, he appeared ready to negotiate, or at least hear more.

"Before I go any further, I would like to tell you what the government is proposing to do, regarding your discovery."

"Proceed," Billings tersely replied.

"Because of the secrecy involved, the government proposes that you relocate. After the initial test of the world's first nuclear reactor at the University of Chicago, most of the work on the A-Bomb was done at Oak Ridge, Tennessee. Your work deserves the same consideration. Like I said before, you will be in charge of the project, code named "Thaumatrope.""

"We used that name based on the 19th century toy and your use of it describing motion perception. As you know, the toy consisted of a single disk suspended from a single piece of string. In most cases, a picture of a bird resting on a branch was on one side of the disk, while an empty birdcage was on the obverse side. When the string was rotated rapidly between the fingers the bird would appear caged, employing the principle of the persistence of vision."

Professor Billings broke into Billings' drone. "I know all of this. My real concern is my work. Where will I work, how much money will I receive and where will I live? Oh, and the recognition of my achievement.

"Let me first say your name will be as well-known as Oppenheimer's if your project is successful. The only reason I was reiterating the facts was for my own benefit. I am not a scientist, but only what you would call a coordinator. I am here to lay out the basics. You and your wife will be considerably compensated and your living accommodations will be equally generous.

"Over the next few days I will setup your banking, the logistics of the move and a cover story for the university; your tenure is guaranteed. And last, your money." Phillips pulled out a small black notebook and pen from the inside pocket of his suite coat. He scribbled down some numbers. After tearing out the sheet of paper he handed it to Billings.

"This will be your monthly salary for as long as it takes you to complete your work and a prototype is constructed"

The professor's reaction was immediate. His eyes widened and mouth dropped slightly as he stared at the slip of notepaper. While Billings seemed to be frozen in thought Phillips abruptly stood up. "By your reaction I can assume that is satisfactory. No need to see me to the door, I'll be in touch." With those words he turned and moved quickly to the door. After partially opening it, he turned to the professor, still immobile in disbelief and said with a smile, "Good day, Professor Billings."

***

Necedah, Wisconsin was far from the cultured world Professor Billings was accustomed to. What it did offer was an ample source of electrical power from the nearby dam and isolation within the Necedah National Wildlife Refuge. His house was located offsite, mostly at the behest of his wife, requiring a daily commute along a single lane of highway plagued by darting dear and impatient truckers.

The buildings were constructed within a double layer of chain-linked fence, topped with razor wire. The security force consisted of a compliment of Army military police from nearby Fort McCoy. Specially configured Humvees constantly circumnavigated the asphalt road that encircled the outer barrier. Patrolling only the outer perimeter, they knew nothing of the workings within the compound. A special division from

Langley, Virginia controlled the internal security.

Mr. Phillips arrived in Professor William's lab and found him in a huddle with several associates. His visits were increasing the closer *Operation Thaumatrope* approached a functioning prototype. When he entered his appearance was noted by the assembly and they dispersed, knowing it was going to be a private meeting.

"Good morning professor," Phillips said, while extending his hand in greeting. "I understand you are almost done with the prototype."

"Good morning Mr. Phillips," he replied and accepted the hand. After all the months both men worked together their greetings were formal and Phillips' first name continued to be a mystery. Even his business card only stated, "Mr. Phillips 703-555-0623" and every time a call was made to that number the operator never questioned him for further clarification.

"Yes, I was hoping an initial test might be accomplished tomorrow morning," he excitingly answered. "Please, come over here to the main console. I want to explain the process and what tomorrow's experiment should produce."

The two men stood before a large window surrounded by a six-inch stainless steel frame. Looking at the glass, neither of them saw anything beyond their own reflection until Professor Billings turned on the lights within the isolated chamber, beyond the thick glass. The room's interior immediately became visible and a substantial sheet of metal stood within its center. In front of the glass partition and immediately below the ledge, a metallic console faced the glittering metal obstacle. The distance between the two was about twelve feet.

"Mr. Phillips, allow me to explain."

"When activated, this device will make any object transparent. When a strobe light is correctly synced with a fan, for example, the fan appears to stop. Without the use of a strobe the rapid movement of the blades gives the illusion of mass. In reality, space exists between the blades as proven when the fan stops.

"Now, on a molecular level, everything we see is only visible because atoms are in a constant state of motion. This is called thermal noise. What this machine will not do is interfere with the atomic structure. It has nothing to do with mechano-chemistry—where atoms and molecules are intentionally altered. Like the apparent suspended spinning fan, frozen in place and because of the reflective light of the strobe, this machine will appear to stop time."

Phillips turned to the professor and said, "Very impressive. Now as I have told you before, I am not a scientist, but what about the heat generated by your device? Wouldn't the rate of fluctuation be so intense that shear friction would cause a total meltdown?"

"Yes, I can see that you have learned a few things during your involvement with the project," he said. Smiling slightly, he motioned to Mr. Phillips to have a seat.

Sitting across from him, Billings began his explanation. "Beyond that glass window, which incidentally is four inches thick, is an airless chamber—a vacuum. Above and below are placed a 'Gravity Generator', in effect creating a weightless environment. Without Earth's gravity and atmosphere the reduction of thermal friction is eliminated. The 'Gravity Generator' was created through the efforts of my university. When we realized the significance of the discovery, it was decided to keep it under wraps for a while." He wryly added, "It even escaped your attention."

Phillips sardonically fired back, "Not so, it was one of your 'breadcrumbs' you left behind," causing the smile on Billings' face to evaporate.

Regaining his composure he resumed, "Okay, when fully activated this machine will scan that piece of steel. The machine is unlike linear X-ray's, computed tomography and magnetic resonance imaging, all of which are used to penetrate soft tissue. The thaumatrope will omit the principle of the persistence of vision and will be capable of real time exploration of solids. I may add, without altering their molecular structure. That chair you are sitting on Mr. Phillips. You are not really sitting on it; in fact, a shell of electrons surrounds every atom. When two atoms come together they have 99.999999999999% of space between them. What we hope to do tomorrow is stop the apparent movement of electrons."

"How certain are you it will be successful?"

"I'm 99.999999999999% certain," Professor Billings smugly replied. "Now I have a lot to do until that time, so I will bid you adieu."

Both men rose, shook hands and parted company.

***

It was a crisp autumn day. Long shadows of pines stretched across the primitive roads of the nature preserve. As Mr. Phillips' car kicked up the gravel they were weakened in the smothering dust of its wake. Once cleared through security he pulled into a nearly full parking lot. Stepping outside of the vehicle he could hear a distinct hum coming from the main building. After entering the noise became more intense.

Professor Billings acknowledged his presence and quickly handed him a pair of noise canceling headphones. Attached to the headset was a throat microphone, which he instinctively strapped around his neck. After positioning them on he was coaxed toward the viewing window.

"I wanted to be ready for your arrival Mr. Phillips. It should only be about ten more minutes before the first pulse is fired at the steel. Because you will not see any molecular change directly, these glasses need to be worn. They are active 3D glasses that contain a liquid crystal that communicates with the system. You may look at any of the monitors," he said and gestured toward the several of them positioned within the lab.

The pitch of the machine increased, aided with the headset, it was only moderately noticeable. Several technicians busied themselves turning dial, making notes and conferring with each other. Mr. Phillips saw their lips move, so they were presumably on other communications channels than the one he shared with the professor.

"Stand by for first pulse," Billings announced. "Five, four, three, two, one—engage!" A power drain was evident by the sudden dimming of the lights. A sheet of paper, placed in front of the steel sheet, began to hover slightly.

"That sheet of paper is a marker to see if the anti-gravity is functional. Although we have devises that tell us the force of gravity at play, we use it simply as a visual aid. It also lacks sufficient mass to prevent any physical damage within the chamber," Billings said, noticing it got Phillip's attention.

"Now look at the monitor, and back again at the steel panel," his voice became electrified. "It's working, it's working! My god it's working," he exclaimed, acting like a schoolboy flying a model airplane for the first time.

The section of steel stood immobile, but the display on screen was a different matter. The seemingly solid piece of metal turned translucent and the test pattern, previously hidden behind the solid mass, became visible. The mood was euphoric, every scientist and technician caught up in the celebratory atmosphere. Suddenly the elation ended.

"What was that?" the professor exclaimed.

While everyone was caught up in the moment, a black flicker darted across the closed-circuit television network. It was clearly something, but too quick to identify. Fearing a possible meltdown of the system the abort command was given.

"Place the system on standby," Billings commanded. "I want to review the video before we continue. Samuelsson, feed the replay into this one," he indicated, pointing at the one nearest him. Samuelsson was on the far end of the lab, and by the color-coded identification nametag, a technician. He responded to the request by adjusting some of the controls at his disposal.

"Okay, whenever you're ready."

All eyes focused on the recording. As the mass began to melt into transparency, an ill-defined form traversed the glowing view of the now see-through steel.

"The phenomenon must be an anomaly. Run it again, this time at a much slower speed," Billings impatiently ordered. Again the nebulous form shifted across the screen. Before it could disappear from view he yelled, "Freeze it!"

Studying the suspended action frame it looked as if someone may have waved a hand, or something, quickly over the camera's lens.

"Let's have a look from another angle. Call up the view from the camera directly over the target."

From the overhead view the steel sheet appeared as a thick silhouette of a bar. The paper, which rested on the floor, began to elevate and move closer to the camera. The camera's timer, visible on the right side of the screen, was rapidly recording the milliseconds of elapsed time. Unexpectedly, the shadowy mass appeared not over the target, but in front of it. Something had indeed moved between the viewing window and test object.

"Samuelson, run the first recording again, this time at a much slower speed. On my command, be prepared to freeze the action. I want the feed to go to all monitors this time. Everyone, watch for anything identifiable." Again, the technician complied.

The recording began, this time at a rate so slow it almost appeared as if it wasn't moving. Slowly, and barely discernable, the blank sheet of paper began to move away from the chamber's floor. When the mysterious object entered into view on the right side of the screen all of the staff stirred with heightened interest. By the time the object reached center view it was apparent they were looking at a human form.

***

Having encountered something completely unexpected, the test was halted and postponed. The following day, the group gathered around Professor Billings and waited for his instructions. Mr. Phillips remained outside the circle, skimming the attendees for their reactions to yesterday's events and wondering what the professor might say.

"Ladies and gentlemen, we are all stunned by the events of yesterday. What we saw, may, or may not, have been a reality. So, today we are going to replicate what was done, only this time at an accelerated frequency." Several hands were raised in an attempt to have some personal concerns answered.

Professor Billings waved down their appeals for recognition and said, "There is no need for speculation at this point. Based on the recordings, what we saw is a reality, but it requires further investigation before we get too carried away with conjecture." Waving his arms in a sweeping motion, he dismissed his colleagues—it was time to begin.

As the group parted, Mr. Phillips steered a course toward the professor. "Good morning Professor Billings," he said, while again embracing his hand in their routine greeting.

"Shall we?" the professor extended a gesturing hand in the direction of the main council, implying commencement of the experiment.

Like yesterday, the lab vibrated after all systems were online. All the staff eagerly watched their assigned controls, occasionally glancing at the nearest monitor, in anticipation of possibly witnessing a great encounter with another civilization. Once the previous velocity of the beam was achieved the professor twirled his right index finger in the air, indicating an increase in the atomic vibration.

Slowly an image of a humanoid being of stout proportions began to materialize on screen. As the rate was intensified the form became more defined. The size of the creature was actually concealed by what appeared to be some type of spacesuit. The faceplate obscured any facial detail, reflecting only the mirror image of the occupants within the lab's interior. Next to the alien sat a large square cube, apparently made of some type of metallic substance because of its reflectiveness. The being raised its right hand in greeting and Professor Billings responded in kind, mesmerized by what was unfolding before his eyes. The sheet of blank paper eventually floated between the lab's window and the unexpected caller.

The paper was snatched from its state of suspension in the weightless environment. Using some form of writing implement, it began to record a message; finishing, the unidentified alien then turning it toward the viewing window.

The words on the paper were beyond belief, "Hello fellow occupants of Earth. Our civilization has predated yours by thousands of years. We always suspected you would come to this point in your development where we would be discovered. Unfortunately, your finding of our existence poses a problem for both our cultures. We cannot coexist."

After holding the paper up to the window long enough for everyone to read it, the co-Earthling released the sheet, allowing it to slowly tumble in mid-air. The creature then began to move sideways, away from the path of the projection beam. The large square cube, however, remained fixed between the sheet of steel and observation window.

In a millisecond, a flash of light spread from the block of metal to completely envelope the entire lab. Soon after, the flood of light overwhelmed the main building, eventually vaporizing all the structures within the double-layered barrier of chain linked fence. The effects of the blast, or rather implosion, never exceeded the limits of the security perimeter.

***

"From NBC News World Headquarters, this is a special report," the off-screen announcer began, followed by a close up shot of Lester Holt.

"Good evening. We have a late breaking report of a crash involving a military aircraft on a routine training flight in Central Wisconsin. The unnamed pilot, the only person aboard the F-22 Raptor, safely ejected the jet before impact. The plane crashed into several agriculture buildings located at the Necedah National Wildlife Refuge. The U.S. Fish and Wildlife Service operates the facility and there were reports of causalities on the ground. We hope to have more information available later in our broadcast."

Lester Holt turned toward a different camera and said, "Now for the other news. The Labor Department just announced—"

THE SECRET

Hands fixed around a hot cup of coffee, Peter Bothesworth leaned forward and asked, "Can you keep a secret?"

Cliff Miller, Peter's friend for many years, going back to their Army days, never demanded a vow of secrecy. Without hesitation he quipped, "Pete, you know I can. Cross my heart and hope to die," he chuckled and formed a sign of the cross over his chest.

They finished their meal at The Sea Chantey Restaurant, one of the many seafood restaurants dotting Boston's coastline. It was next to a marina and at this late afternoon hour, there was little activity. They had selected a comfortable corner table, sheltered from the sea breeze that offered some privacy. Most of the other patrons sought the inside warmth of the restaurant. The bumping sound of boats hitting the piers with the clatter of halyard clips against aluminum masts provided a backdrop to dinner. An occasional gull's cry interrupted the rhythm of both tide and wind.

Peter sipped his coffee, leaned back and began his story with cautionary words, "This must never be revealed beyond this conversation." Cliff nodded and wondered what he'd blindly agreed to.

"Before our Army days and right out of high school, I decided to hitchhike cross-country. It was one of those Route 66 ideas planted in my adolescent brain from watching television. Against my parent's protests, and common sense, my trip began from Boston. With money from my grocery store job, I outfitted myself with an Army surplus backpack, boots, sleeping bag, canteen, mess kit, poncho and other essential items.

"Well, it was early June; I thought the trip would last a couple of months, at most. My end game involved a return either by bus or train." Peter shifted in his seat, sipped his lukewarm coffee and grimaced.

"The first day out was great; clear skies and a light breeze. I made good progress through a series of rides and pleasant weather conditions. My first notable ride came from an elderly couple, which proved most unusual. I was a bit surprised I even got a ride from them—in view of the fact older people tend not to pick up strangers. They showed interest in my life and were pleasant people. In three hours or so I told my life's story and goal of hitchhiking across America. They dropped me off and as I got out of the back seat the elderly woman reached in her purse and pulled out some money. Forcing it into my hand she said, 'Here son, something to make your trip a little easier.' Needless to say, this was unexpected and it threw me for a loop."

"I tried to refuse; the more I declined the more insistent she was. I reluctantly accepted and waved goodbye. Another odd thing about them; they made a U-turn and headed back in the direction we came from. They struck me at the time as odd. In doubt of the reality of the gift, I watched them disappear and counted two hundred dollars. Yep, ten twenty-dollar bills, and nested in the wad of cash was a strange medallion, or coin."

Cliff's face brightened in disbelief and said, "Damn! That's like getting over fifteen hundred bucks in today's dollars."

"You bet," Peter agreed, forming a steeple with his hands over the rapidly cooling coffee. "I also found the coin of particular interest. It had no markings or apparent value, only concentric circles around what appeared to be a pyramid. I assumed it to be a good-luck charm, shoved the money and coin deep into my jean's pocket and moved on.

"The extra money didn't alter my plans to find out-of-the-way retreats, abandoned buildings or secluded woods as rest stops. Adding the money to my grubstake gave me the confidence I would not starve. Having camped before, I was no stranger to living under the stars, but those were short outings. The actuality of an extended trip began to hit home after only two days. The scent of spring in the air and fair winds appealed to me, but the reality of less-than-favorable conditions brought me back down-to-earth.

"Encountering my first storm I was fortunate to find an abandoned outbuilding. The shed, with its furrowed grey boards aged from years of neglect with lateral exposed breaches, offered some refuge. The roof was equally in disrepair with curled asphalt shingles practically devoid of its granular covering, scoured from water runoff. I kept dry using my poncho as an improvised tent. Lulled into sleep from the irregular dripping sounds of the rain, my slumber became a gateway to apprehension.

"I had a most unusual dream." He waved a hand in the air as if to erase the comment and said, "No, not a dream, it was a nightmare."

"You know some dreams are almost forgotten soon after waking. Well, this wasn't the case. Even today it bothers me," Peter said reflectively. He then motioned to one of the waitresses indicating a refill of coffee.

"It started with being forced along a long corridor in search of something. It was either fear or something else that propelled me. My journey was not voluntary. I had a sense of descending and my steps slanted forward, almost to the point of tumbling into an unseen abyss.

"I found myself in a large circular room made of stones, not evenly sized and without a defined circular structure. Nebulous, is all I can say about my surroundings. The irregular surface offered an escape, steps jutting out from the walls, which seemed to pulsate with an ever-changing dimension. Yet, I was able to move upward, sometimes walking, and sometimes crawling."

Peter paused while the waitress filled his cup and Cliff's. A slight fog hung over the hot brew due to the chill coming in from the harbor.

Taking a sip of hot coffee he continued.

"I ascended the interior at full speed and woke up," he raised both his hands into the air like a magician who suddenly produced a bunch of flowers. The waitress, who had previously filled their cups, now busied herself on the terrace lighting the stainless steel patio heaters.

"Well Pete, so far your story doesn't require any secrecy. Some of this stuff you already told me when we were in the Army together. Unless you tell me the elderly couple tried to get back the money and accuse you of stealing. Is there more to this yarn?" He sat back and appeared annoyed.

Peter grinned. "When I told you some of this years ago, I glossed over much of it. Believe me, it gets worse." Cliff's eyes brightened with the prospect of something greater than being accused of stealing.

"I woke up in a sweat, really stressed by the dream, so real; I had difficulty shaking the vision, expecting evil waiting for me at the top of the structure. I pushed it from my mind and concentrated on resuming my trip. Almost dawn, I grabbed some of the canned food from my backpack and hurried through breakfast.

"Throughout, I avoided the major cities, preferred the secondary roads which offered more seclusion and easier access to remote campsites. Although camping outdoors was always free, my experience with rain and no running water made me reconsider hotels. Ma-and-pa type motels offered the best value. I got a room after my next day's travel. I made excellent time between hiking and rides. By evening I located a small motel with a string of row cottages that faced the highway.

"The cabin was small; room for a bed, dresser, and sink, no television, just a radio. A shower stall in the bathroom with toilet, gave me barely enough room to stand. Though cramped, after several days on the road, it was heaven. The motel also had a laundromat, so I was able wash my dirty clothes.

"My personal chores done, I settled down on the mattress, lumpy—but better than the sleeping bag. The periodic pulsing sound of passing cars along the thoroughfare sped past my window. Turning in, the radio's music of Patsy Cline overpowered the external rush of traffic and I fell into a deep sleep."

Now their coffee cups were half empty and Cliff suggested switching to something with a little more kick. Peter agreed, "I'll have a double scotch whiskey on the rocks." Cliff nodded likewise. The waitress took their order and left. Peter resumed.

"My dream from the night before returned. It continued where the last one ended. I found myself on the top of the building, or whatever it was; people walked along a pathway in continuous procession. Unaware of my presence, they kept their eyes fixed on the person in front of them; men and women of all ages—no kids though."

Peter stopped while the waitress placed their glasses in front of them. Both reached simultaneously for their drinks.

Peter continued, "Suddenly, everyone turned in my direction. All their eyes were on me. Without a word, they raised their arms and pointed toward me. From the recesses beyond the ring of people, a dark figure emerged. It was without form, possessing a nebulous presence everyone in the group seemed to acknowledge, first by the parting of the circle; later as their collective eyes followed until it stood before me. I was on the inside catwalk of the building. It had no hand or arm, but sensed a part of it was reaching out to me. Recoiling from its grasp I fell backward into the chasm and awoke with a start gasping for breath before I could hit bottom.

"The wall clock read 3:30; the radio produced dead air static. I shut it off and instantaneously fell back asleep. Thankfully, It was a dreamless, and I awoke again as the dawn filtered through the window. Following a hearty breakfast in the restaurant across the street, I got lucky. My next lift took me a little way past Omaha.

"This ride came from a trucker who liked to talk my ear off and listened to country-western radio stations. Annoyingly, the signals faded in and out as we traveled down the highway. It was a small price to pay for the ride. Most of the time I nodded in agreement and occasionally offered a reply.

"My trucker friend was called Bill. I still remember his name because he said, "'Name's Bill, Wild Bill Bable.' It certainly fit him."

Cliff appeared irritated, "Wait a minute. What about the dream? Does it have anything to do with this story you're telling me?"

Peter smiled, reassured his friend, "It's central to my story. You'll see." He took another drink of scotch from his glass and continued.

"Okay. Now this trucker, Wild Bill, pulled into a truck stop a little west of Omaha. He was driving north to the Dakotas, but before leaving me, he talked one of the other truckers into giving me a ride further west. At the time I appreciated his effort. His recommendation pulled more weight than my thumb hanging over a highway.

"One nice thing about some of those truck stops is the convenience of showers. The ride said he needed to get cleaned up before moving on, so using the opportunity; I paid for a shower room too. It was small; one side a changing area, the other side shower. A strong smell of Pine Sol permeated the interior. From inside the room I could hear the boisterous exchange between drivers, their exploits, some sexual in nature, and destinations. The locked door gave me a secure feeling for backpack and myself. Once cleaned up, I hurried out to the truck yard and found my ride waiting to hit the road.

"I don't remember the driver's name. He didn't have a distinctive name like Wild Bill, and his personality was more introverted. Although his silence was uncomfortable, it gave me an opportunity to rest. I used my jacket as a makeshift pillow. I nested my head between the window and back of the passenger's seat, and quickly dozed off. The same dream from a day ago began to replay.

"This time I walked in a circle and apparently ran from someone or something. The moon appeared in my dream as a slender crescent. Midpoint in the sky; from my vantage point it was partially obscured by a windmill's wheel and tail assembly. My position changed. The moon behind me now, cast a dim light on the corroded structure. It hid behind the windmill again. This went on and on, always within a short distance from the rusted shell, almost dizzily, I continually circled its metal skeleton.

"I awoke again, troubled by the dream, tried to engage in conversation with my trucker buddy; he curtly replied to my questions, but didn't take the bait for more exchange. I watched as the telephone and power line poles fled by the moving countryside, occasionally nodded off, but in my semi-slumber, dreamless."

Several of the restaurant's patrons wandered outside to view the approaching sunset. Peter and Cliff remained seated on the east side veranda, a spot favored by those seeking the morning sunrise. Soon the sky would change from its lilac hue to dusty brownish-orange. Finally the red and auburn overspread of sunset would succumb to indigo, bestowing the heavens with a glittering array of stars.

"When mister-no-talk dropped me off south of Denver in a little town called Castle Rock, I realized I neglected to call home since leaving Boston. I found a pay phone and called collect. My lack of communication did cause them some anxiety, but my call relieved them of the worry. I told them of my travels, but left out the disturbing dreams. Knowing my mother, she would have said it was a bad omen. After saying my goodbyes I searched for a place to eat, having accepted the fact that my trip depended heavily on restaurants and lodgings. My culinary abilities were no match for diner cookery.

"Once in the upper elevations of the West, the night temperatures became colder and I was concerned about the consequences of sleeping under the stars. I located a restaurant, ate a hearty meal of eggs, sausage and pancakes. I developed a craving for coffee; it was hot, sweet and creamy, warmed my insides, and gave me a caffeine jolt.

"Castle Rock couldn't have been home to more than a thousand people and my presence aroused some curiosity. I thought it best to seek some higher ground outside town. I found a suitable shelter under an outcropping a short distance from town, although the ground was a bit hard. I gathered firewood and built a fire for the night, which required constant attention. My sleeping bag was more suited to the campgrounds out East, than the higher elevations of the West.

"As the embers of the fire slowly died I stared up at the stars amazed at their beauty, I felt small by comparison and wondering about my future. Beyond the fading glow of my camp I heard rustling noises and tried not to think of what caused them. I managed to get some sleep, although little, it was dream free. Next morning I heated a can of beans. It wasn't as good as a restaurant meal, but hot. I broke camp and attempted to hitch a ride.

"Several cars rocketed past me, leaving me literally in the dust. Finally a rancher, I noticed earlier going north, now south, gave me a ride. He had me jump into the back of his green, 1941 Chevy stake truck. I knew it was a 1941 model because he proudly proclaimed its age after he dropped me off in Pueblo, Colorado. 'This old beater will probably outlast me,' he yelled as both driver and truck rumbled away.

"The ride to Pueblo was close to two hours in his 'old beater,' I inhaled much of the eighty some miles of dirt along the way too. After dusting off, I looked for a restaurant to freshen up and throw some water on my face."

After taking a drink of scotch, Cliff said, "So far this is a yarn about a kid heading out West and nothing more. Oh, ya—and strange dreams."

"You're right, but now we are getting into the strange stuff—besides the dreams, of course."

Peter picked up his glass of scotch and downed it. He caught the waitress' eye, signaled a refill with a sweeping motion of his index finger between their glasses. In a hushed voice he resumed his story.

"Pueblo was a lot bigger than Castle Rock. Probably ten times, I guess. This might be a nice spot to rest; I thought and enjoy the scenery at a slower pace, rather than from a truck window. I had enough money at this point, but wanted to conserve my funds, so I looked for a reasonably priced place.

"Many newer buildings occupied the town, a result of the great flood of 1921. The Arkansas River swelled its banks, killed over 1,500 people and almost wiped out the entire town. Most striking was the large amount of bars. Walking through town I got a few probing looks. Hikers were not uncommon, but viewed with suspicion—a touch of xenophobia, I guess. Considering this, I lucked out and found a rooming house reasonably priced on the north end of town, near Highway 50. It would be a good spot to start from after a couple of days of rest. I saw the silhouette of the mountains on the western horizon. This was not going to be easy.

"I hung around Pueblo for a couple of days mentally preparing myself. I felt anxious and questioned my decision to leave Boston. Putting self-doubt aside, I considered my next move. Now it became more of a quick mission to get to the west coast and accept the routine of motel, restaurant and ride.

"With the help of a free gas station map I planned an itinerary based on time and terrain. I spread the map on my bed, noticed the next destination, Montrose, Colorado was over 200 miles away; I'd be challenged by winding roads and uncertain conditions. Chances for a ride would be best at a truck stop; so on the day of departure, I ate breakfast in a gas station catering to truckers.

"I found the next ride without any trouble. In fact, a trucker came up to me and asked, 'Want a ride kid? I'm going as far as Montrose.'"

"He must have overheard my conversation with the waitress and my travel plans. I grabbed my stuff and followed him to an old 1955 Peterbilt with elongated hood, exhaust stack on the passenger's side and high cab that loomed in front of me. It was brown, matching the rust on the rest of the truck and dulled from being blasted by desert sand. The tires were bald, but the worst part of my ride was the 10,000 or so gallons of gasoline sitting behind me.

"I threw my rucksack on the floor of the cab, climbed aboard and prayed this was not going to be a ride I'd regret. Between the grinding of gears, both on the up shift and down shift we were forced to shout. Even with the yelling, I was happy for the small talk, because it kept my mind off the thought of riding on a gasoline bomb. After five hours I sighed with relief, when he dropped me off in the center of town. I thanked him for the ride and looked for a place to eat. My stomach grumbled more than the truck's engine, part from hunger, and part from swallowing exhaust fumes.

"I spotted Montrose city hall, which was an imposing structure with its four-storied brick building. I surveyed the town and noticed a restaurant across the street from City Hall. Several cars parked nearby usually indicated good food. A red neon sign in the front window boldly proclaimed, "Eat" and I needed no further invitation. I looked forward to a seat that didn't bounce and vibrate.

"I tucked my backpack and bed roll under the table of the booth, grabbed a menu, ordered food, and consulted the map again. Montrose was about 270 miles from Gallup, New Mexico and route 66. I guessed Gallup to be a five or six hour drive."

"The waitress placed my order to the side of my map and asked, 'Where you going kid?'"

"I told her of my plan to hook up with Route 66 and head west. She laughed and told me, 'You'll probably get a ride to Cortez easy enough, but don't count on getting one from Cortez to Gallup.'"

"I asked 'why?' She said, 'Why? That's the Devil's Highway, and nobody picks up strangers on Route 666.'

"She began to tell me of the strange happenings along its 135 miles.

"'Some call it The Antichrist Road,' she said, then told me several stories which would keep any rational person off that highway.

"'One person swore a truck headed straight for him, down the middle of the road, with sparks and flames flying from its wheels—going over 130 miles an hour—or so he claimed. He drove his car into the ditch to avoid being hit. Some say it's a road cursed by a wicked medicine man. Sometimes a shaman appears in the backseat, startling the driver into losing control. There are tales where a coyote would appear in the road, only to change into a man—or man-like creature. I think they call them shape-shifters. Anyway kid, that highway should have a sign on it; drive at your own risk.'"

"Now your story has some meat on it," said Cliff. He motioned the waitress for a refill and leaned back in his chair, folded his arms over his chest and eagerly waited to hear Peter's resumption of the narrative.

"After she left I pulled my plate close to me and begun to eat. By that time my meal had grown slightly cold, which forced me to gulp down my lunch. Between mouthfuls I glanced at the map, seeing if there was another way to Gallup. Actually, there was another route, but it would take me back to Alamosa and highway 285—too far out of my way.

"Darkness loomed. A bit spooked by what the waitress said, I spent the night in town to start fresh the next day. My check came, I asked for a recommendation of a reasonably priced motel. Leaving her a nice tip, I followed her advice. Her recommendation fair; one's idea of nice doesn't always match your own.

"I was determined to get an early start and avoid any chance of night travel on *The Devil's Road*. After a substantial breakfast in the same restaurant, I was on the trail again.

"My first ride came from a couple of rich college bound kids driving a blue Corvette convertible. Enticed like me, about the adventure along Route 66, they could have been from the casting department of CBS studios. I figured they were all about using their pretend TV personas to pick-up girls—they had the looks and car to boot. By mid-morning one of the guys offered me a beer, which I declined. I got nervous when both of them started to drink. My traveling companions said they were going as far as Mesa Verde National Park to 'check out the scene.'

"It was over a three hour drive, interrupted by several stops to switch drivers and get rid of the used beer. I offered to drive, but they declined. Probably feeling it was better to drive drunk than let a sober stranger take the wheel. When we reached Mesa Verde my nerves were totally shot and I was eager to part company with *Tod and Buz*.

"Before hitching another ride, I had lunch at the usual gas-station-tourist-center-truck-stops. The food was as bad as the service and I was happy this would be a one-meal town. Once outside, I hoped to find a ride to Gallup. While making my way among the parked vehicles I received one rejection after another. It wasn't the idea of giving a vagabond a ride; it was giving a vagabond a ride with their family.

"'Not having much luck, are you Bud?' said the driver of a Red Indian Motorcycle with attached sidecar. Dressed in faded jeans and wearing a windswept brown bomber style leather jacket, he sported a matching leather helmet—the kind of helmet worn by World War II aviators. He wore distressed heavy buckled black boots with cleated soles and rounded heels. Each step he took toward me kicked up a small dust cloud, adding a layer of dirt to his already grime-caked biker' boots."

"'I'm going to Gallup. Want a ride?' he asked.

"*A rides a ride*, I thought. The cycle, nearly as old as me, maybe older, was painted red but had lost its luster years ago. Big too, a large headlight hung over the front fender cowling, which covered half of the balloon tire. The same type of shell also enveloped the rear tire. I wasn't crazy about the openness of the sidecar and it was barely spacious enough for my things and me. He handed me a pair of goggles saying, 'You'll need these Bud.' After I put them on we roared south, down Route 666, in broad daylight.

"With Cortez behind, a mountain range on our left side grew larger as we thundered down the highway. The rising sun silhouetted the mountain range and the sky slowly changed from flushed to pale azure with wispy cirrus clouds. To the left a large rock formation resembled an enormous building being pushed to the surface; a massive mound of earth surrounded its base. And that's the last thing I remember before getting to Gallop."

"What happened? Did you fall asleep?"

"I don't know what happened. That's what's so strange; the last thing I remember was the rock formation. Not only did I lose all recollection of the rest of my trip; seven days of my life were unaccounted for."

"You lost seven days?" Cliff asked in amazement. His body leaned forward from the announcement, both arms rested on the table for a moment. He tried to comprehend the validity of the remark.

"I didn't realize I lost seven days at the time. I hopped out of the cycle's sidecar, thanked my goggled speckled driver, and looked for a place to eat. I was finally on Route 66. Gallup was a reasonable sized, possibly 10,000 people but with an overabundance of eateries and gas stations. Many cars traveled that highway, drivers had to fuel up and eat; I guess it was logical, considering the traffic. One that displayed a big red sign labeled; Virgil's, Vegie's or Virgie's—or something like that— captured my attention.

"Legs stiff from the tight ride in the cycle, I ambled over to the restaurant, thinking it was the same day after leaving Cortez, only three hours later. The first thing I noticed, besides the attractive waitress, was a calendar behind the cash register. There in bold black and white print, "today's date" proclaiming the day as being exactly one week after leaving Cortez.

"I chose an empty booth, dropped my bag and bed roll onto the window seat, and sat next to it. My first instincts made me flip open the flap of my rucksack and retrieve my cash. I kept the money below the table off to the side and made a quick count. To my surprise, not only was money there, I was richer, but not sure by how much. Somewhat uncomfortable recounting the money, I saved it for the privacy of my motel room—when I got one.

"Having cash in my wallet, I didn't need any money from the bag. With damp hands I quickly rolled up the bills and put them back. I asked myself more questions. Having all that dough made me tense.

"*What the hell happened to me? Did I rob someone, get knocked out in the process and lose my memory? Did I become an accomplice to a robbery—or worse, maybe murder?* My mind tried to come up with an explanation for the absence of time and unaccounted money.

"After the attractive waitress took my order I asked if the date on the calendar was correct. She said, 'You bet sweetie,' smiled and walked back toward the kitchen. I blushed slightly, both for asking the unusual question and because she called me 'sweetie'"

"You sure had a lot of unusual—" Cliff paused a bit in search of the word and said, "shit."

Peter finished his scotch; somewhat watered down from the melted ice cubes, and raised it in the direction of the passing waitress. She acknowledged his silent request with a smile.

"After my meal I went to the rear of the restaurant to call my parents on the pay phone. I hadn't talked with them in quite a while and I also needed the reassurance I was sane—or confirmation of even having parents. I omitted the part of my newfound wealth. Hell, I didn't want them thinking I was now a criminal.

"Their voices helped lift my spirits. I found a motel a little off Route 66. Locked my room, propped a chair under the doorknob as a precaution and dumped the entire contents of my bag onto the bed. I watched as several bills spilled out among my clothing and canned goods. I counted over eight hundred dollars. I shoved most of it into one of my socks, rolled another one over it, and stuffed it into a bottom corner of the knapsack. I repacked the rest of my belongings on top, and realized something was missing. The coin was gone! Although it had no real value, the fact it was missing, plus a week of my life, led me to suspect foul play. Why would I have all this money and lose an apparent worthless coin? Coincidence? Maybe.

"I had a restless night, full of strange fantasies similar to those of a few weeks earlier. In part of the dream I was in the center of a large group who seemed to either be teaching me something or asking questions; I wasn't sure which. Once again the windmill appeared. It turned wildly in the full moonlight. Shadows of people danced on the ground, but there were no people, only phantom shadows. The evening air was hot and the turning blades of the windmill squealed while the nocturnal dance of discombobulated shapes grew in intensity. I awoke dripping with perspiration.

"Staring up at the ceiling, I knew the tail-end of my journey would be by bus. Enough of the hitchhiking, I thought. After a shower, clean clothes and I was ready for breakfast, and a way out of town. As it turned out, the restaurant served as a bus stop and would be along in about an hour."

The waitress brought out drinks, gave a quick smile to both of them and departed.

"From Gallup, I spent the night in Flagstaff then made my way to Barstow, California. This last leg west stretched from Barstow to Los Angeles. I spent a couple of wild days in LA before heading back, by train.

"Los Angeles in the early 60s was crazy. I spent a lot of time at Muscle Beach, near the end of Santa Monica Pier. For a guy from Massachusetts, LA seemed like sin city. That is where I met Phyllis. She was just one of the many hard bodies that hung around the beach scene. Everyone there was preoccupied with having fun, from the health-and-fitness group to the extroverted exhibitionist who put on spontaneous acts. Phyllis and I fell in love. I vowed to return, which of course, I never did.

"Phyllis and I parted ways on the train station's platform. Leaving town with an aching heart, I traveled on The City of Los Angeles, a train that unfortunately doesn't run anymore. My trip from the west coast to Chicago was uneventful, except for the fantastic scenery along the way."

"Those were the days," Peter Bothesworth reflected with a look of satisfaction. "You could travel in class, observation cars, fully reclining seats, dining cars and bathrooms. I was flush with money—well, at least in my mind. I now enjoyed leisurely travel, seeing America in first class accommodations. I have to admit the mystery money continued to gnaw at me.

"From Chicago's Union Station to Boston's South Station was only a day's travel. Once in Chicago I called my parents so they could pick me up. Of course they were glad of my safe return and relieved in my homecoming. It was a great adventure, but glad it was over too."

Cliff Miller spoke before Peter could say another word, "Hell, I can understand why you may have wanted to keep the finding of the money secret, but that's well over 50 years ago. I doubt someone might come after you over the money now."

"Cliff, I had to tell you the complete story before the rest of my tale made any sense. You'll understand my need for secrecy once you hear the rest. Actually, you may think me crazy.

"Before getting involved in any career, or school, I enlisted in the Army as my next adventure. That is where we met during the end of my three-year enlistment. Because I volunteered and not drafted, I was able to choose my duty station. The Army was more indulgent with the volunteer, as opposed to the draftee; I was able to stay in Massachusetts, selecting Fort Devens as my duty post. I used my time wisely, worked towards a college degree, eventually earning a Master's Degree, post discharge.

"Okay, this part of my life you pretty much know about. Now I am going to tell you something you don't know about me. A few weeks ago, a man who made an appointment through my secretary, dropped the equivalent of the atomic bomb on me. He began by introducing himself as Mr. Cochran, told me of my trip out west, Highway 666, loss of time and the money."

"After all those years!" Cliff exclaimed in disbelief.

"Yes, it certainly was a shock. Hell, he even knew about the elderly couple and the money from the lady. I sat there dumbstruck. He told me I was chosen."

"I asked, 'chosen?'"

"At this point I asked him if the dreams had anything to do with all this. He told me, 'Your mind was being surveyed to see if it'd be a good candidate. That elderly couple were scouts.'"

"'Was everyone part of the plan or mission?'" I asked.

"'Yes, everyone except those college kids that gave you a ride. They had us worried for a while.'"

"He told me during my lost week I was programed. When I questioned him on the programing he said it wasn't taking away my freewill. It was like making my brain's receptors more efficient and capable of retaining a greater amount of information. Unknown to me, my progress was monitored. According to Mr. Cochran, it's 'time to collect the data.'"

"What about the coin, Pete?" Cliff asked incredulously.

"Turns out it was some kind of tracking device. After my 'programing' it was no longer necessary."

"Shit! Pete, you are right, I am finding this hard to believe. Is this one of your cockamamie jokes? If it is, you sure took the long route getting there."

"I wish it wasn't true—let me finish." Peter's eyes were glazed and Cliff studied Pete for a moment.

"The group came from another planet or galaxy. They certainly were not from planet Earth. I wasn't the only one this happened to. Although I never knowingly met anyone else, I'd only had Mr. Cochran's word. He told me I'd be transported back to his planet where the "download" of all of the information and life experiences acquired over the years would take place. It's to be a one-way voyage.

"I told him in no uncertain terms he's nuts, and I'd not be going willingly. He told me I had no other option. If I went willingly my transit would be pleasant and my family cared for, otherwise not so.

"It seems his race selected that spot to kidnap people, my words not his, because of the folklore and legends surrounding the area. Any unexplained disappearance or unusual occurrences would be attributed to The Devils Highway. They probed humans before, but earlier methods never gave the complete picture of our species. They needed more of a recording device. What better apparatus than the human brain? It required some modifications. Because they are patient beings, time was not important as results."

Peter reached into his inside jacket pocket and pulled out a long manila envelope and placed it in the center of the table. Pushing it toward Cliff he said, "Here is a large sum of money, you will need it to help out my family during the investigation of my death."

"Death!" Cliff gasped.

While Cliff sat in stunned silence, Peter continued. "They arranged an evening ride for me at sea. I will have an unfortunate accident—fall overboard. When Sarah calls she will be concerned why I haven't returned from our dinner meeting. This is the hardest part, the loss of my beloved Sarah and the agony it will cause. Your natural reaction will be to call the police. By that time I will be far away and nothing you or the authorities do will change the plan. My body will not be recovered."

"What the hell plan you talking about Pete?" asked Cliff, still in shock over the sudden revelation.

"I will not leave behind a suicide note and foul play will eventually be eliminated as a reason for my death. The large amount of money you now have comes from my abductors, to prevent any audit trail; this could arouse suspicion of something planned. I'm telling you all this because I need help for my family, through the turmoil of my passing. After a time they will receive a life insurance payout too.

"I am going to be picked up there in a little while," Peter Bothesworth pointed around the corner of the building to the dock, barely visible through the evening's blackness. It's all I know. The story you will tell the police is that I arranged a nighttime trip into the bay. You will tell the police nothing more. Even if you did tell them, no one would believe you. In fact, they'd question your sanity. Apparently my sponsors, if you can call them that, will provide a collaborating story. You are the only person who knows the truth."

Peter Bothesworth rose and dropped a wad of money onto the center of the table. After taking one enormous gulp of his drink he shook Cliff's hand, who remained sitting in disbelief. "You've been a damn good friend and I will miss you too," he said before turning toward the harbor.

Cliff rose from his chair and watched his friend slowly walk away. Peter paused and turned toward him, gave a thumb's up sign, and resumed his pace in the direction of the stairs. Peter was gradually engulfed by the night.

Cliff moved closer to the deck's handrail, straining his eyes for any movement in the night. The darkness was slightly interrupted by the wide spaced row of lights along the pier. The distant growl of a boat approaching the yachting marina became louder. Red and green navigation lights bobbed back-and-forth, advancing, they grew in magnitude. The lone shadowy outline of a man leapt from pier to boat. The noise abated for a few minutes, intensified; then the roaring of the engine faded, along with the running lights, into places unknown.

ABOUT THE AUTHOR

Christopher Malinger lives with his wife Eileen in Central Florida. His most recent work, *The Object of Desire*, appeared in *Journeys VII; An Anthology of Award-Winning Short Stories* published in 2014. He is also a winner in the Florida Writers Association Adult Collection, Volume 7, *The Sweet Scent of Spring; published in 2015.* Other works include a collection of short stories, *Tales to Keep You Awake, The Back Roads of Terror,* and his novella, *The Wabele.* He is a member of AWP-Association of Writers & Writing Programs and the Florida Writers Association.

www.christophermalinger.com

www.ingramcontent.com/pod-product-compliance
Lightning Source LLC
Chambersburg PA
CBHW070530130626

46555CB00003B/1343